Colour Blind

Bullets & Shells Don't Discriminate

G.S. Willmott

Explanation of Ranks and Infantry Organisation

Throughout this book terms will be used which may be unfamiliar to the reader.

Infantry Groups

Platoon — 24 - 48 men comprising 3 to 4 Sections

Company — 120 men comprising 3 to 4 Platoons plus HQ support.

Battalion — 700 - 800 men comprising 3 to 4 Companies plus HQ support.

Brigade — 3000 - 4000 men comprising 3 to 4 Battalions plus HQ support.

Division — 12000 -14000 men comprising 3 to 4 Brigades plus HQ support.

Corps — 30000 - 40000 men comprising 3 to 4 Divisions plus HQ support

Infantry Ranks

Colonel: Commanding officer in an Infantry Battalion.

Brigadier: Commands an Infantry Brigade.

Major General: Commands an Infantry Division.

Lieutenant General: Commands an Infantry Corps.

General: Commands an Infantry Army

Field Marshal: Commands many Infantry Armies

In the Beginning

Chapter 1

The First Australians, the Aboriginals, arrived in Australia over 50,000 years ago. Having left the African continent, they made their way down through Asia and eventually undertook the first open sea crossing in human history. They discovered the landmass now known as Australia, which then included New Guinea. This was a vast continent comprising megafauna, rain forests, deserts and glaciers. The skeleton of Mungo Man, dating back 42,000 years, reveals amazing details about early life and spiritual belief systems. The Aboriginals were accomplished stonemasons, hollowing out rock into important spiritual monuments with ground edged axes. They engraved the world's earliest maps and made the first image of the human face. Tribal networks soon crisscrossed the land and innovations in art and technology such as the spear and boomerang, spread rapidly. An art style known as the Archaic Face can be found over thousands of kilometres, right across the deserts of Western and Central Australia. The first Australians occupied almost the entire continent, and they flourished, as evidenced by oral histories and engravings across the country. This is the time when Dreamtime came into being.

For thousands of years, people lived with Australia's strange and ferocious megafauna like the six-metre giant lizard megalania and the marsupial lion.

Megalania

Marsupial Lion Hunting Mega Kangaroo

Twenty thousand years ago a new ice age engulfed Australia; its effects were devastating, not only on the megafauna, which largely became extinct but also on the indigenous population. Sea levels dropped to one hundred and thirty metres below the current level and deserts expanded to cover ninety per cent of the continent. Average temperatures dropped steeply; they were six degrees colder than the current average. The worst drought in the continent's history made the living for both beast and man extremely difficult. These extreme conditions lasted over ten thousand years.

During this period forests disappeared, animals became extinct, and the vast majority of Australia had no fresh water.

The Aboriginal people gravitated to areas that had access to water such as rivers. This restricted the size of the population, as the areas for habitation were limited.

Australia changed from a land of plenty to a very hard and inhospitable environment.

Recent scientific studies using radiocarbon dating of archaeological sites have highlighted the distribution of people across the landscape over aeons of time.

The findings, published recently in *The Journal of Archaeological Science*, suggest that about 21,000 years ago, almost all people in modern-day Australia migrated into smaller areas, abandoning as much as eighty per cent of the continent. The result of this dramatic consolidation was a reduction in the birth rate by over sixty percent.

People noted every water source and passed the information on through song lines – the oral transmission of important cultural and spiritual information. This information codified into The Law and was the blueprint for survival through ten thousand years of drought.

About 14, 000 years ago, the temperature began to rise, and plant and animal populations returned to the levels of earlier years. This allowed indigenous people to once again extend their area of influence across much of the continent.

These fluctuating temperatures also produced large variations in sea levels, which in turn had far-reaching consequences for Aboriginal communities.

At one stage, during the ice age, sea levels were approximately one hundred and thirty metres below their present level, and, what is now mainland Australia was connected to modern Papua New Guinea and Tasmania.

With the rising sea level, these land masses separated, with the profound effect of isolating Tasmanian Aboriginal people from their mainland relatives.

Tribal Life
Before The White Fella Came

Chapter 2

Kunaggai Tribe – Ha Region 1800

The Kunggai tribe were a proud people; their ancestors arrived in the Hawkesberry River region approximately thirty thousand years before the first white man stumbled across the fertile wetlands. Gidga was seventeen; he had been initiated as a man of the tribe a few years before and wore the Bora belt.

The Bora is the name given to both the initiation ceremony of young male Aborigines and the site where the ceremony takes place. The actual ceremony is both sacred and secret and differs from Aboriginal nation to Aboriginal nation. The initiation involves the learning of sacred songs, stories, dances and dreaming cumulating in the actual ceremony.

Bora Ceremony 1898

Gidga was now regarded as an expert hunter and a good husband to his wife Kaawa and father to their first-born son, Kumba.

The area was plentiful with wildlife such as kangaroo and wallaby as well as possums and bandicoot. Rich vegetation kept the tribe nourished with various berries and bush fruits.

Gidga also created bark canoes for himself and members of his extended family. He would regularly navigate the vast waterways, catching an abundance of fish and scraping oysters and mussels off the rocks. All in all, the Kunggai people lived extremely well as their ancestors had done for thousands of years before them.

Canoes were constructed of a single sheet of bark tied together at the ends with vines. Bark used to make the canoes came from several trees.

The bark from grey or swamp she-oak, bangalay, and stringybarks such as *Eucalyptus agglomerata* and *Eucalyptus acmeniodies* were used.

Gidga was leading a hunting party on the far side of the river when they came across the strangest sight. Six men with strange white skin were rampaging their way through the scrub cutting the undergrowth with some magical stick. Speaking loudly in a dialect unknown to Gidga and his companions this strange band of men was heading their way. Gidga instructed his men to hide and observe this group and try and ascertain if they posed a threat. The white men passed by the Aboriginal hunters not knowing they were being watched, Mani, the youngest of the group, stepped on a broken tree limb which made a large cracking noise, alerting the white men of their presence. The leader of the group, Ben Fogarty, turned, raised his rifle and shot the young boy. The other strange men followed suit. Only Gidga managed to escape. That day changed the way the Kunggai people lived forever more. The white man had arrived.

Gidga waited for the murderous group to move on. He then made his way back to the tribe's camp, ever mindful of the chance he might run into this ghost-like group of creatures again.

Once back, he called the tribe together and described what had happened and how strange white men with fire sticks had slaughtered five of their best. The elder of the tribe, Akuna, listened intently to Gidga's story. He did not ask a question or make a sound. Akuna stood up holding his hunting spear and instructed ten of the tribe's best hunters to take their spears and follow him.

They were embarking on a hunting expedition; not for game, but to exact vengeance.

The indigenous band of brothers set out to track their quarry. After following the white man's trail of severed branches and broken tree limbs they smelt smoke about an hour from their own camp.

Gidga was assigned by Akuna to scout ahead and report back with his observations. He heard men's voices and laughter he crept closer to their camp and saw six white men sitting around a campfire and passing a bottle around. Each man would drink from this strange-looking receptacle and pass it on to the next man and so it went around the circle.

Gidga observed this ritual for over an hour. As time went on the men got louder and louder as they drank more of the magic water or whatever it was. He decided to report back to the chief. He slipped back without a sound and made his way to where his mob was waiting for news. Akuna instructed his party to follow Gidga to where the murderous mob was camping and eliminate everybody without mercy.

Gidga arrived at his observation place and noticed the six men were now sleeping around the fire.

'We sneak up quietly until we are on them, then we spear them until we are sure they are all dead.'

The white men didn't know what hit them; within minutes they all lay dead with their blood flowing like rivulets towards the campfire, creating a heavy acrid smoke.

The garrison commander in Sydney Town, Lieutenant Jefferies, dispatched a group of twelve soldiers to find the missing group after they failed to arrive back from their Hawkesbury expedition. They discovered the remains of Ben Fogarty's group one hundred kilometres from Sydney, overlooking the magnificent river they set out to map. Although all the bodies were badly decomposed it was obvious that natives had killed them.

After returning to Sydney with the explorers' remains, Lieutenant Jeffries assembled a force of one hundred men to hunt down any Aboriginals they could find within a one hundred mile radius and eliminate them. This he thought would prevent all future attacks against the colony's population. He was very much mistaken. Attacks against the white settlers continued for many years to come. Indiscriminate attacks by the white invaders also continued.

By the early 1900s, the Aboriginal population around Sydney had decreased to a few hundred people. Most were living in humpy villages enduring squalid conditions. In 1901 Australia became a nation in its own right, having achieved independence from Great Britain. Unlike America, there was no war of independence; just a negotiated agreement. Most Australians, including the government felt a very strong loyalty to the mother country.

War Declared
All Able-Bodied Men Should Answer the Call

Chapter 3

Gidga's great-great-grandson, Jimmie Pearson, was a very proud man, proud of his cultural heritage, proud of his family and proud to be Australian. Jimmie was not an Australian citizen. None of his mob was, as Aboriginals were denied citizenship. He and his kind had no say in who would govern the country. Nor could they enjoy a beer after work; in fact, they had very few rights.

Jimmie was chatting to his workmates on the building site in George Street where he was working on a fifteen-storey skyscraper. It was their lunch hour.

'Hey, Frank what do you think will happen over in bloody Europe?'

'Fucked if I know, Marty, it seems there's a lot of sabre rattling going on since that Prince Ferdinand or whatever the fuck his name was got knocked off.'

'They reckon it could be the start of a big bloody war and as sure as eggs, Britain will jump in. Any opportunity to trounce bloody Germany.'

'Well, if Britain declares war guess who's gunna follow quick smart?'

'Australia of course.'

'Would you sign up, Marty?'

'Probably, what about you?'

'Bloody oath, I'm sick of hauling concrete all bloody day.'

'What about you Jimmie?' asked Frank.

'I reckon I would.'

August 4th, 1914

Britain declared war on Germany, and the Commonwealth countries, including Australia, declared war on the same day.

The three mates wandered down to the army recruitment office after work on Friday, November 16th, 1914.

Frank was the first to be interviewed if you could call it that.

'How old are you, mate?'

'Twenty-two, sir.'

'Fair enough. Go and join that line over there for your medical.'

Frank passed the medical with no problems; he signed his papers and for all intents and purposes he was in the army.

Marty was next up and, like Frank, he passed the medical and signed up.

One more to go. Jimmie stepped up; he wasn't asked for his age. Just one question needed to be answered.

'Are you a bloody Abo son?'

'I'm an Aboriginal.'

'Really, where are you from? Redfern, I bet.'

'That's right, Redfern, Sydney, Australia. My family has lived there for thirty years, and before that, in the Hawkesbury region for over thirty thousand years.'

'Don't get bloody smart with me, black fella, you're an Abo, and we don't take Abos, so piss off and go and spear some kangaroos. Next.'

The three good mates went over to the Paddington Green pub opposite the recruitment centre for a beer. Jimmie was only allowed lemonade. Jimmie said nothing of his rejection until they sat down at the bar.

'Well cobbers, it's off to war we go. I hope we're all in the same division or battalion or whatever the fuck they call it,' said Marty.

'I won't be; they rejected me,' said Jimmie.

'What! Did you fail the bloody medical mate?' asked Frank.

'They don't take Aboriginals apparently.'

'You've got to be kidding.'

'Nope, we're not good enough to be able to fight for our country.'

'That's bullshit,' said Marty.

It wasn't bullshit; the Australian Government on advice from their army generals decided that no Aboriginals would be enlisted on the basis that the white diggers would object to fighting alongside them.

Frank and Marty began basic training three weeks later. Jimmie went back to the George Street building site. The building he was working on, the AMP Centre, had slowed down as more than half the workforce had enlisted.

The two cobbers fronted up to Holsworthy Army Base on Monday, December 15, 1914, to undertake six weeks basic training. After the first week, both agreed on how it got the name of basic training. They learned how to march in time, the correct way to make a bed and how to march double time. Both Marty and Frank were billeted in the same hut and their bunks were side by side.

'Hey, Frank do you think the Germans will be impressed with our marching ability?'

'Mate, they'll be shaking in their boots when we march by. I also think we'll impress the shit out of them with our nice shiny boots.'

'Seriously, when are they going to teach us how to fire a fucking rifle? I would have thought that would be an elementary skill for a soldier about to go off to war,' said Marty.

'I'll just be happy when they issue the buggers so we can see what they look like.'

They didn't have to wait too much longer; by the third week, arms training had begun, and all recruits were issued with Lee Enfield 303 rifles with bayonets attached.

The boys learnt how to use the sights and load the magazine, but most importantly, how to fire and hit a target. An essential part of their training was learning how to dismantle their 303, clean it and then reassemble it. In the conditions they were likely to encounter, a clean gun could save their lives.

Their embarkation orders came through on February 5th. They were to set sail on the SS *Ceramic*, bound for Egypt.

Marty and Frank were loaded onto a train leaving for Circular Quay along with about two thousand other blokes. On arrival, they marched from Central Station to the waterfront where the SS *Ceramic* was waiting to take them to war.

Conditions on the one-time cruise liner were cramped, to say the least, and the only activities to break the monotony were cards and two-up, a gambling game using pennies.

After six weeks of seasickness, boredom and trepidation, the *Ceramic* docked in Alexandria. As the diggers disembarked they began to sway and bump into each other, and it was evident they had not yet found their land legs. The First Battalion was ordered to assemble. They were then ordered to march to the train station, bound for Cairo.

'Geez mate, aren't you glad we learnt how to march in basic training?'

'Bloody oath, Marty, although it would have helped if they trained us marching through a fucking blast furnace.'

'Yeah, I know what you mean. It's bloody hot here. Having sixty pounds on the back doesn't make it an easier, hey?'

After marching for twenty miles they arrived at the central rail terminus and loaded onto carriages for the four-hour journey. The troops arrived in Cairo at about 5 pm and were then ordered to march to Mena Camp, which would be their home for the next month or so.

Mena Camp

'Well mate, I never thought I'd ever see the bloody pyramids in my lifetime, and now they're in our bloody backyard.'

'Yeah, it seems crazy Frank, I can hardly wait to climb one of the buggers.'

'Me too, I'm also pretty keen to experience what Cairo has to offer if you know what I mean.'

'Yeah, I see what you mean mate, but we have to be pretty careful. That demo on the ship by the ship's doctor on how they treat the clap looked pretty frightening.'

'Yeah, I'll be wearing a franger no fear. Do you know what they call them here?'

'No.'

'Englishmen's overcoats.'

'I thought they'd use their bowler hats.'

'I keep thinking about poor old Jimmie, poor bugger; he really wanted to be with us.'

'Yeah, I know what you mean, Marty, I think about our cobber a lot too.'

The two Aussie mates became tourists, climbing the Great Pyramid and taking camel rides. There were other benefits also; they could go into Cairo, a city like nothing they had ever seen before.

Marty and Frank had only seen Sydney, so Cairo, with its diverse population and nightlife, was something to behold.

'Hey, Marty! Come and have a look at this.'

Marty came over and looked inside the small café.

'Have you ever?'

There were several men smoking large water pipes and watching a belly dancer going through her motions, so to speak.

'Do you wanna go in and give it a burl, mate?'

'Why not?'

Both Frank and Marty took a spot on some big fluffy cushions; the Arab who ran the show introduced himself as Rebu.

'Would you like some coffee and a shisha?'

'What the bloody hell is a shisha, mate?' Marty asked.

'It is a water pipe. See, everyone has one. You will like it; very relaxing.'

'Bloody hell, mate, I could do with a bit of relaxing with what we've been through lately. 'It's not going to cost us an arm and a leg is it, Rebu?'

'Excuse me, sir?' Rebu was confused. 'I don't want your arm or leg, just a pound each.'

They both laughed.

'It's just an expression we use in Australia, meaning expensive.'

'Oh, I see,' said the café owner, starting to become impatient. 'Well, would you like a coffee and shisha?'

'Yeah, why not? You only live once as far as I know.'

Rebu departed and came back fifteen minutes later with two very exotic shishas.

'I have selected a very fragrant tobacco for you,' said Rebu. 'It is mixed with strawberries, apple and grapes. I am sure you will enjoy it. I will bring your coffee shortly so relax and enjoy the dancer and your shisha.'

'If the boys down at the rugby club could see us now!'

Frank broke up laughing and agreed.

As they smoked their unique blend and sipped the coffee that Rebu had brought them, they did feel relaxed. The belly dancer was quite pretty although quite chubby; she danced in front of them, shaking all the flesh she could, smiling the whole time.

After about an hour, Frank and Marty decided to move on and find somewhere they could have a drink. They found a very rowdy bar full of Aussies and poms.

They ordered a couple of beers and started to chat with the other diggers and a couple of the poms. Things were going very nicely until a pompous British captain walked in with a pair of military police and closed down the bar for the night.

Marty couldn't help himself and started shouting. 'You pommy bastards are always trying to ruin our fun! You can't play cricket, and you can't play football, and you can't fight either!'

Marty then turned on his heels and bolted out of the bar, running down laneways and ducking under awnings with the two policemen giving chase. He finally lost them in the night market. He then tried to find his way back to Mena without being spotted. He sneaked in around midnight and lay down on his stretcher. Frank had been back for nearly two hours.

'Where the fuck have you been you silly bastard? You could have been thrown in the slammer if they'd caught you,' said Frank.

'They were too fucking slow mate. They couldn't catch a cold in a thunderstorm.'

'Yeah, well you'll have to watch yourself. They'll be out looking for you next time we go to Cairo.'

'Yeah, I know. By the way, are we going in again tonight?'

'You're insatiable.'

'Well, are you up for it?'

'Is the Pope a Catholic?'

'That's the spirit; I wish Jimmie were here. He would have loved Cairo.'

'Yeah, he'd be up to his ears in it.'

'So, what I've heard around the camp is the district we need to go to is called Wassa. That's where all the brothels are.'

'Right, well we better bring our Englishmen's overcoats with us,' said Marty.

'Too bloody right, we don't want our dicks to drop off before we have a go at the Huns,' replied Frank.

'Have you got any idea how much to dip the wick?'

'I've heard about one pound for thirty minutes,' said Frank.

'Jeez, they know how to charge then,' complained Marty.

'Don't worry mate; it'll be money well spent.'

'I bloody hope so. I've got a confession to make, Frank.'

'Oh yeah, and what's that then?'

'I'm a virgin.'

'You're not.'

'Yep, never done anything with my willy other than taking a piss.'

'Guess what? So am I, so we're two virgins about to be introduced into the world of the flesh.'

The both roared laughing and gave one another a bear hug.

'By the way, we better make it a goodie. I've heard a rumour that we're about to ship out,' said Frank.

After mess, the two excited diggers made their way into Cairo and headed straight for the Wassa district.

The date was April 2, and they were in for a big disappointment. They picked the day the Battle of Wassa was fought.

First Battle of Wassa was the appellation given to the first of two riots in the Haret el Wassa involving the ANZACs. The ANZACs had received news that their period of training was at an end. Orders had been received for them to embark on the long-awaited action at Gallipoli.

Causes of this disturbance reportedly lay in a desire to exact revenge for past grievances arising from dealings with the district's denizens. These complaints included diluting liquor, exorbitant prices, and high rates of venereal infection. There were also rumours of stabbings of ANZAC soldiers by locals.

Trouble began soon after five o'clock in the evening when soldiers began evicting whores and their pimps into the street and tossing their possessions out after them. Bedding, furniture, clothing and even pianos were thrown from windows of buildings several storeys high. These materials were piled in the middle of the road and set alight. Military police from the Australian 9th Light Horse Regiment came on the scene and tried to evict the soldiers from the houses being attacked. Five arrests were made, although fellow ANZACs refused to let these men be taken away. Four of the prisoners escaped.

British military police were summoned. About thirty came charging in on horseback. They were abused and showered with stones and bottles by the disgruntled soldiers. The MPs fired their pistols over the heads of the rioting crowd, wounding four. This only served to further inflame matters and forced the police to withdraw hastily. Efforts by the Egyptian fire brigade to douse the bonfires were also frustrated, its hose-lines were cut, its members manhandled – especially after they turned a hose on the crowd. The engine itself was finally pushed into the flames.

The unrulier elements began to loot some shops and set fire to a Greek tavern. Shortly after seven o'clock, a second fire engine arrived, this time under cavalry escort, which exercised extreme tact, and the various fires were tackled while a still sizeable crowd looked on. The 'Wassa' was close by Shepherd's Hotel, where the Australian commander, General Birdwood, had his headquarters, but he could do nothing to quell the riot. Eventually, armed troops were called out. After Lancashire Territorials were drawn across the road, the rioters wisely began to disperse, and order was eventually restored by ten o'clock.

Burnt Out Buildings After Battle of Wassa

A formal inquiry was convened the following day under Colonel Frederic Hughes, commander of the AIF's 3rd Light Horse Brigade, to investigate the causes of the riot and establish responsibility for its outbreak. Many New Zealand officers attempted to disclaim that their men had played any part, although the evidence of their presence was quite conclusive. The Australian officers were adamant that New Zealanders not only took part; they predominated.

The damages bill of £1,700 was equally shared between the Australians and New Zealanders.

A few months after the first battle of Wassa the second battle occurred. It was very similar to the first as many Australians and this time only a few New Zealanders rioted over the same gripes, prices, prostitutes and diluted alcohol.

High command stepped in and ensured there was entertainment for the troops in Cairo.

Frank and Marty stayed away from the riots although they could empathise with the troops.

A popular song sung by the ANZACs was:

Land of heat and sweaty socks,
>Sin and sand and tons of pox,
>Streets of sorrow, streets of shame,
>Streets to which we give no name;
>Harlots, thieves and pestering wogs,
>Stinks and dirt and sneaking dogs,
>Flies that drive a man insane,
>Make him curse with oath profane:
>Blazing heat and aching feet,
>Gyppo guts and camel meat,
>Clouds of choking dust that blind,
>Drive a man clean off his mind;
>The Arab's heaven – soldier's hell,
>Land of Bastards, fare thee well!

In fact, the whores of Cairo were not beautiful women with magnificent bodies, which could lure a young soldier and seduce him with her womanly charm.

'They tended to be a motley assortment; none of them was physically attractive. Their faces were hastily daubed with paint and powder, and the best one could say of them was that they looked the part – blowsy, all of them. One, a blonde, might have been in her early twenties; a couple of others, brunettes, would have been passable had they been properly turned out. As for the others: they were human nonentities – and very frightened.'
     William Turner AIF

Frank and Marty encountered total desolation as they endeavoured to enter the red light district.

'Shit mate, I don't think we're going to be lucky tonight. Let's get out of here before they try and arrest us,' said Marty.

'Yeah, I think we better get back to camp quick smart.'

Aftermath of Wassa Riot

Frank, Marty and their comrades in arms did a bit more than play tourists during the Egyptian posting. They were ordered to march from Cairo to the Suez Canal in forty-degree heat across the desert with a full pack. Many dropped from heat exhaustion; the remainder arrived completely exhausted. McCay, the Australian General, had ordered the march to toughen up the diggers before they were shipped off to fight. He was widely criticised for this ludicrous exercise.

Orders had been received by High Command to ship the Australian and New Zealand troops (ANZACs) to invade Turkey landing at a place called Gallipoli. British and Indian troops were also involved.

Winston Churchill proposed to break through the Dardanelles – the narrow sea passage from the Mediterranean leading towards the Ottoman capital, Istanbul, and the Black Sea. His plan was not accepted by the whole of cabinet and the military, but after seven weeks of rancorous debate, he prevailed.

Frank and Marty were, at last, going to see some action; they were both excited and nervous about the prospect of fighting the Turks. Neither of them had even heard of Turkey before, let alone Gallipoli.

They were herded onto a ship called the "HMAS *Armidale*".

Departing for the Great Adventure

April 24th, 1915

A flotilla of troopships escorted by warships sailed off to Gallipoli. The next day, the 25th, would be the day they landed; a day that would go down in the annals of history.

'Hey Frank, this is the best tucker we've had since we joined the fucking army.'

'Yeah, it's bloody good. I hope it's not like the last meal they give somebody before they hang the poor bastard.'

'Yeah, I know what you mean, mate. Anyway let's get stuck in, it may be the last fucking meal we ever eat.'

'Don't say that.'

The young ANZACs rested as much as they could, but it was difficult when the bloke next door was snoring and farting, and there was nowhere to move.

About two in the morning, the officers moved around among the men, waking those who were sleeping and giving words of encouragement to those awake.

The instruction was they were to climb down rope ladders into the boats. These boats would be towed in close to shore, and then they would be rowed for the remainder of the distance.

April 25th, 1915 3.30 am

The time had arrived.

Frank and Marty slowly lowered themselves down into the landing craft, which was rocking quite severely.

'Right mate, we're on our way to fame and glory.'

'I don't know about that Marty.'

'I'm just kidding mate. How are ya feeling?'

'Yeah, okay, Marty, but you make sure you stick by me mate, we've got to protect each other's arses, right?'

'You bet Frank; no worries.'

As the boats began to get towed towards the shore there were only muted whispers among the soldiers. After about forty very long minutes they were cast off to make the remainder of the journey on their own under oars.

There was an eerie silence as the landing boats slipped through the sea. The only sound was the water lapping the sides of the craft.

The silence was broken by the sound of Turkish rifle fire.

'Shit, they've spotted us. Can't be too many of the buggers if that's all they can throw at us!' the officer in charge of the craft exclaimed.

With that, a cacophony of gun and cannon exploded around them. Bullets were hitting the boats and the water. They also were hitting the young, inexperienced soldiers from a faraway land.

'Keep ya fucking head down, Marty.'

'Don't you worry mate. I bloody well am.'

Marty felt a warm, slimy substance running down his face.

'Shit, I think I've been hit.'

'No, you haven't, it's the bloke next to you It's his brain.'

'Holy fuck, the poor bastard.'

Marty wiped the grey material from his face with his army-issued handkerchief.

They were getting close to the beach. Bodies were floating everywhere, and the Turks were blasting them from all sides.

The water had turned red.

'Right men, out you get and give them hell,' the officer shouted.

He used a leather megaphone so he could be heard over the battle noise.

'Remember, we've got to stick together, mate,' Frank yelled.

'You bet, Frank.'

They both jumped out, one after the other, and sank into the chest-high water. They found it difficult wading through to the beach with their heavy packs while holding their 303 rifles above their heads, but they both made it. Many didn't.

Anzac Cove

The two diggers ran for the craggy cliffs, hoping to get some cover from the relentless onslaught. They lay against the cliff face and looked up. They couldn't see a bloody Turk. They just heard the sound of their machine guns and shells.

Their commanding officer, Lieutenant Roberts, crawled up to them.

'Lads we need to start making our way up the cliffs to establish a secure position.

Frank and Marty looked up again, and Frank whispered, 'How the fuck are we supposed to get up there? Abdul has got us covered; as soon as we stick our necks out, the bastards are gunna blow our heads off.'

Roberts moved among his men. 'Okay, let's get up there and give Johnnie Turk some of his own back, boys.'

They had no choice; the platoon started up the sandy cliff. The rocks crumbled from under their feet making progress almost impossible. The Turkish onslaught continued unabated, and many ANZACS fell. They reached a plateau, and it was here where they would remain for the next twenty-four hours.

A shallow trench was dug, giving them some protection but not much.

'You know what Marty? I don't think Jimmie's missing out on much.'

'Yeah, I reckon he's better off in his lounge room of his Redfern terrace.'

Eventually, the Turks started to pull back from the ridges under heavy Allied shelling. This allowed the Australians to progress to a more secure line and dig more substantial trenches. For the next eight months, they fought the Turks with many thousands from both sides dying.

August 6, 1915

One of the most significant and famous assaults of the Gallipoli campaign, the Battle of Lone Pine was intended as a diversion from attempts by the New Zealand and Australian units to force a breakout from the Anzac perimeter on the heights of Chanuk Bair and Hill 971.

The Anzacs shelled the overcrowded Turkish trenches for some hours before the charge. The Anzac forces, consisting of 1st, 2nd, 3rd and 4th Battalions entered the main Turkish trenches within half an hour. The 5th, 6th, 7th, 8th and 12th Battalions reinforced the First Brigade the next day; the battle raged for four days.

The Turks had established a labyrinth of log-covered trenches, and it was in this environment the two sides fought. There was total confusion and amid screams of anguish and despair, Lone Pine became a furious nightmare of hand-to-hand combat.

'We were like a mob of ferrets in a rabbit warren,' one Anzac said. *'It was one long grave, only some of us were still alive in it.'*

Frank and Marty were trying to see in the dark, putrid Turkish trench. Their mate George was with them. They had fought their way to this position and now were hell-bent on ensuring there were no Turks left to hinder their progress. Their objective was the end of the trench where they suspected there was a group of Turks throwing bombs at the advancing Anzac troops. By the sounds of it they also had a machine gun.

'Okay, Marty, I think we're all right. Abdul seems to have fallen back. You, George and I need to sneak up on the bastards and throw the Mills bombs down to the end of the trench.'

'Okay, but I can't see George. He was with us a while ago.'

'Shit, we need three of us to pull this off, me to throw the bombs and you two to cover me with rifle fire. We better backtrack a little and find him.'

The two mates retreated through the trench even though it was dark and full of smoke. They found George sitting down against the trench wall.

'George, get up you slack bastard. We've got work to do.'

The soldier didn't respond. On closer examination, they could see blood oozing from his chest where he had either been shot or stabbed with a bayonet. As they knelt beside their comrade, a Turkish soldier leapt out from the dark, thrusting his blood-stained weapon into Marty's back. Frank immediately retaliated with a 303 bullet through the Turk's forehead. Both soldiers dropped to the floor of the trench, no longer breathing.

Frank was devastated losing his best friend, but he knew he couldn't stay to grieve over his mate. The novice soldier knew it would be difficult without rifle cover, but he had no choice. He moved forward, knowing it was highly likely he would be the next one to meet his maker. He slowly approached the end of the trench where he could see daylight and several Turks including the gunner. He crawled along the floor of the trench until he estimated he was within range. The Mills bomb was the first grenade to be used in war; it had a seven-second fuse once the pin had been pulled. Frank pulled the pin on two bombs consecutively and waited until four seconds had passed before he threw them.

Both bombs exploded pretty much at the same time, killing several Turks. The survivors exited the trench as fast as they could only to meet extensive rifle fire from a group of Anzacs who were planning an assault on the Turkish position.

The mission had been successful but at what cost?

Frank continued to take part in the bitter fighting.

Hundreds of ferocious one-on-one struggles broke out in the maze of trenches. Turks killed Turks and Anzacs killed Anzacs in the confusion. Both sides hurled bombs at each other, which were lobbed back and forth until they exploded. The Turkish trenches were lined with the bodies of the dead and wounded from both sides.

Trench at Lone Pine

August 7th, 1915

The following day the 5th, 6th, 7th, 8th and 12th Battalions reinforced what the boys from New South Wales had achieved on day one.

The first day's battalions had been successful in capturing the Turkish trenches so it was just a hundred yard sprint. There were no machine guns to greet them, but the Turks were shelling no man's land heavily, and many fell.

For the next three days, the Turks, intent on retrieving their lost territory, blasted them with heavy artillery.

At the cessation of The Battle of Lone Pine the Anzacs sustained 2,273 casualties, while the Turks lost between 5000 and 7000.

Marty and George were buried at Lone Pine Cemetery.

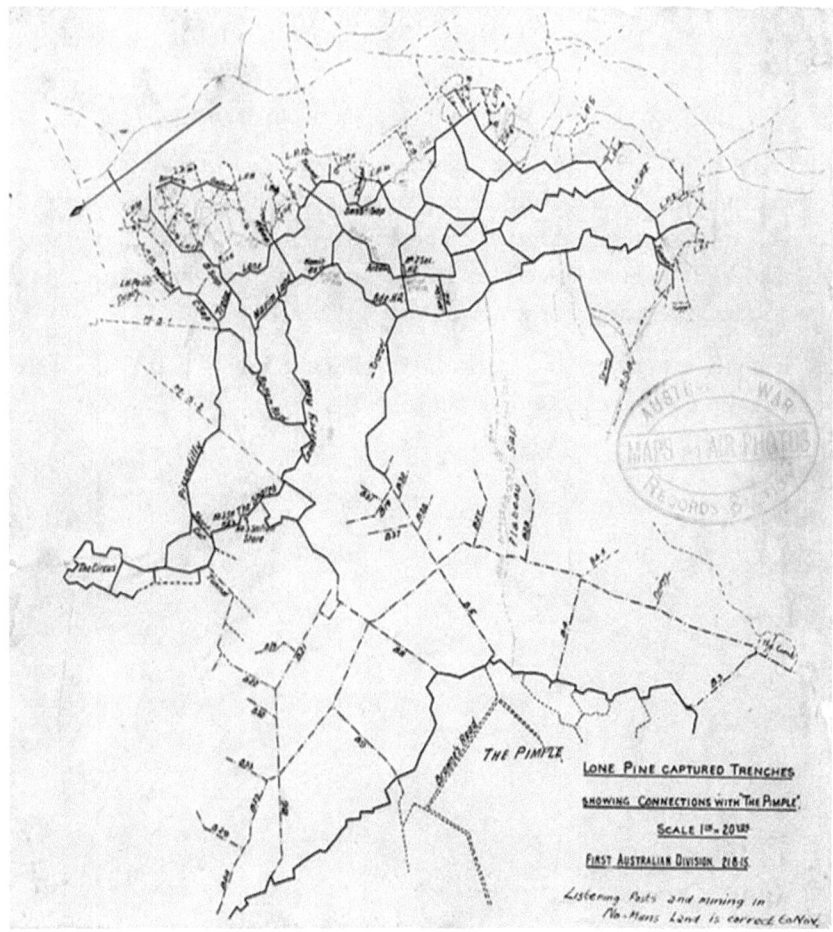

LONE PINE CAPTURED TRENCHES
SHOWING CONNECTIONS WITH THE PIMPLE.
SCALE 1IN = 20YDS
FIRST AUSTRALIAN DIVISION 21.8.15

Christmas was approaching, and the weather was getting very cold. Snow had begun to fall.

Frank had befriended another bloke in the battalion. His name was Tom, and he was from Ballarat, a real country boy. The two got on very well.

'Frank, do you think we are ever going to leave this godforsaken place?' asked Tom.

'Fuck, I hope so Tom, I don't want to end my days here; I am looking forward to dying when I'm eighty-something and the grandkiddies will be standing around my bed waiting for their inheritance.'

'Yeah, me too.'

An officer heard the conversation and approached the two diggers.

'I don't think you need to worry too much fellas. You may be out of here sooner than you think.'

He was right.

On January 8, 1916, Allied forces staged a full retreat from the shores of the Gallipoli Peninsula, ending a disastrous invasion of the Ottoman Empire. The Gallipoli Campaign resulted in two hundred and fifty thousand Allied casualties and greatly discredited Allied military command. Roughly three hundred thousand Turks were killed or wounded.

The Gallipoli campaign was only the beginning. Frank and Tom were to experience more bloody battles in other lands.

They sailed off to France to join their comrades on the Western Front.

Private Jimmie
Aboriginal Warrior

Chapter 4

Jimmie heard of his good mate Marty's death when he ran into Marty's brother at the football. Jimmie was devastated. He was also determined to get over there and shoot the bastards that killed his cobber.

He had heard a rumour that if you told the enlistment officer one of your parents was white, they'd let you in. Worth a try he thought, so he presented himself at Paddington Barracks once again hoping he didn't run into the bastard who interviewed him the first time.

He noticed waiting in line a couple of mates from Redfern waiting to be interviewed. They were full bloods.

'G'day, Lionel how's it going mate?' asked Jimmie.

'G'day Jimmie, so you're joining up too?'

'I bloody hope so; they knocked me back last time for being an Aboriginal.'

'Yeah, well you know the drum don't ya? You just tell them you're a half-caste.'

'Yeah, so I heard.'

'Okay well, I'll see you once you get through.'

'See ya, Jimmie. Good luck.'

Jimmie waited in line until he was invited to step up to the enlistment desk. He was relieved to see the nasty bastard wasn't there.

'Well, son, let's start with your name and age.'

'My name is Jimmie Pearson, and I'm twenty-four, sir.'

'Very good, and your race?'

'I'm part Aboriginal, part white, sir.'

'Which of your parents was white, son?'

'My father sir, he was Scottish.'

'Was he? Well you'd be entitled to wear the clan kilt. What clan did he belong to?'

Jimmie swallowed hard and decided his father belonged to the Mackenzie clan on the basis he had a schoolteacher in sixth grade who was a Mackenzie.

'The Mackenzie clan, sir.'

'Really, that's a strong clan. My clan is McDonald. Okay, son, go over there and join that line to get your medical.'

Jimmie tried not to grin as he walked over to join the line. He passed the medical and was enlisted into the 30th Battalion often referred to as the Scottish Battalion. The 30th wore the tartan of the British Army 42nd (Black Watch) Royal Highland Regiment.

Jimmie couldn't help seeing the irony.

The young black Scotsman began basic training three weeks later.

Basic training was shortened considerably due to the urgency to dispatch fresh troops to the Western Front after the disastrous Gallipoli campaign. Jimmie and his new mates learnt how to march, polish their boots, make their beds correctly and fire the Enfield 303 rifle. Bayonet training could be taught on the ship while making their way to France.

Jimmie was polishing his boots when another digger approached him.

'G'day mate.'

'G'day,' Jimmie responded.

'Are you from Redfern in Sydney?'

'Here we fucking go again. Mate, not all Aboriginals live in fucking Redfern. We're spread across the whole of Australia. In fact, we came to Australia about forty thousand years before you white fellas.'

'Whoa, don't get me, wrong mate, it's just that I played rugby league for St George, and I reckon I could have played against you. If I remember correctly, you played five-eighth for the Rabbitohs.'

'Sorry cobber, I get a bit sensitive about my race considering I'm in the minority around here. That, and the fact they knocked me back to join first time around because I'm what they call an Abo.'

'You're kidding me. I thought they were desperate to enlist every able-bodied man to fight.'

'They are if you're white.'

'Well, as far as I'm concerned I don't give a fuck what colour you are. By the way, my name is Louis most people call me Lou.'

'Pleased to meet you, mate. My name is Jimmie and yeah, I did play five-eighth for the Rabbitohs.'

From that moment on Jimmie and Lou became inseparable.

The two mates and the entire 30th Battalion received their orders to embark on a fleet of troop ships bound for Egypt. Jimmie and his newfound mate boarded the HMAT *Karoo*, a ship leased from the English for the duration.

The voyage was made without incident, and they docked at Alexandria on June 2nd, 1916.

The battalion then marched in the searing heat with a full pack to Mena Camp on the outskirts of Cairo.

The boys did what all the other soldiers had done before them when they received leave; they climbed the great pyramid and ogled at the Sphinx. They also gazed at the painted ladies in the red light district of Wassa. They both decided to leave well alone and wait until they reached France before enjoying themselves with the ladies of the night. While at Mena Camp they were further trained in marksmanship, throwing Mills bombs and bayonet practice. They now felt confident that they could handle themselves adequately when they encountered the enemy. On July 1, 1916, they boarded the *Karoo* yet again, bound for Marseilles in France. Once they arrived, they were immediately loaded onto a train, which took them to the once picturesque town of Ypres in Belgium.

Jimmie and Lou were amazed at the devastation of Ypres. The once famous Cloth Hall and Cathedral lay in ruins.

Australian Diggers Marching Past the Cloth Hall

The 5th Division, including Jimmie's battalion, was given a day's rest before embarking on their next adventure – Fromelles.

The Battle of Fromelles

The Battle of Fromelles started on July 19th, 1916, and lasted until the following day. The battle was an attempt to stop the Germans moving troops away from the Fromelles sector to take part in the Battle of the Somme, which was being fought fifty miles to the south. The area around Fromelles was seen as a "quiet" sector where the Germans could move their troops around with ease without encountering strong enemy fire. The battle was an attempt to force the German High Command to move more troops to Fromelles from the Somme battlefield to support their existing troops.

On July 19th Australian and British troops from two divisions – British 61st Division and the 5th Australian Division, attacked German positions. The lines had been shelled for seven hours by two hundred thousand artillery rounds. The original plan was to shell the Germans for seven days.

The artillery barrage was, however, wasted; British intelligence had failed to discover that the Germans had moved back over two hundred metres and constructed concrete bunkers housing nests of machine guns. The shells had been hitting empty trenches while the Germans were drinking tea and playing cards below ground waiting for the shelling to cease. Once all was quiet, they knew that was their signal to man the bunkers and supporting trenches.

The Australians and British expected very little resistance. After all, they thought, who could survive such an onslaught?

When the Allies attacked, they were hit by a German artillery bombardment that left many allied troops dead in their own trenches. Those who made it over the top faced well dug-in machine guns and turrets such as Sugar Loaf, a massive concrete bunker with machineguns on three sides.

The British 61st was hit badly, forcing them to retire to their own lines after suffering heavy casualties. The Australian diggers did significantly better, reaching what they thought were the German front line, only to find the trenches flooded and indefensible. By July 20th, they, like the 61st, had to retreat after suffering very high casualties.

The Battle of Fromelles was a complete disaster, badly planned and mismanaged by the British High Command. Generals Haig, Haking and Australian General McCay had blood on their hands but made no apologies.

Of the six thousand five hundred Australian troops deployed in the battle, ninety per cent, five thousand five hundred and fifty-three, became casualties. One thousand five hundred and forty-seven British troops – about fifty per cent of those involved, were also casualties.

Many men lay wounded in no man's land crying out in pain from horrendous injuries, despite this; a plan for a temporary truce with the Germans to allow the wounded to be collected was vetoed by senior British officers.

One of those lying dead in the mud was Private Harold Daniel. He was only nineteen. He would never meet his nephew, Garry Samuel Willmott.

Fromelles was one of the worst disasters to befall the Australian Army in the whole of World War One, and it did a great deal to sour relations between British and Australian senior army commanders.

Torres Strait Islander

Chapter 5

Alfred Barnes was a full blood Aborigine from the Djabugay tribe in far north Queensland.

The rainforest around Kuranda, inland from Cairns, had been home to the Djabugay-speaking people for over 10,000 years, under the protection of Bulurru. In Djabugay Country, "Bulurru" was the spirit of creation, the sacred past, the word and the law to be followed. As the Bulurru ancestors journeyed across the land, stories, songs, and ceremonies were recorded and were passed down from generation to generation.

The greatest ancestor of all was Gudjugudju, the Rainbow Serpent. Gudjugudju transformed into Buda: dji, the carpet snake who created all rivers and creeks of the Barron Gorge National Park. During the wet season, Gudjugudju's presence was most profound in his rainbow form. The voice of Bulurru, the creation spirit, could be heard through Gudjugudju in the sound of thunder. Linked by a network of trails through the rainforest, Aboriginal people had an intimate knowledge of their environment and the country's food. Traditionally, they moved along these trails taking advantage of seasonally abundant foods; and were skilled in making tools, clothes, blankets, and shelters from natural materials.

Djabugay Warriors 1800s

1900s

Before European settlement, Kuranda village was known as Ngunbay, or the place of the platypus, an important camping, hunting, and fishing area for the Bama (rainforest) people. However, this all changed with the opening up of the hinterland for gold and tin mining. As Europeans descended on the land, access to the tracks of the Bama people was developed as trading routes that had an immediate impact on the Djabugay people. Many of these trails have been developed into highways, roads, and modern-day walking tracks.

Coffee, the region's first cash crop, began in 1896. The Bama people were soon utilised as farm labourers on the rapidly expanding plantations around Kuranda, until well into the twentieth century. Many Bama became fringe dwellers on the edge of white settlements, unable to hunt and fish or move around as they had for thousands of years.

Alfred Barnes came from the Djabugay tribe; one of the Bama people. He didn't live on the fringes of Cairns. He lived in a neat two-bedroom cottage with his wife Elsie, a Torres Strait Islander. Alfred, or Fred as he was known, worked on the docks as a labourer for two shillings a day. Although the pay was meagre, he enjoyed the work and had made many friends, both black and white. He was more than aware there was a war going on in Europe and most of his white friends had enlisted to fight for their King and country. He was also mindful of the fact that as an Aborigine he was excluded from joining up.

In 1916 most of the talk on the docks centred on the failed Gallipoli campaign and how Australia had lost over eight thousand men. Considering the Cairns population at the time was about ten thousand, of which five thousand were males, these casualty figures shook the close-knit community.

Alfred was keen to enlist, although leaving his beloved Elsie did concern him. He had discussed with his wife the prospect of enlisting as a Torres Strait Islander as they were being accepted.

The two of them had just finished their dinner, and Elsie was making a pot of tea.

'Elsie, I'm still keen to enlist and do my bit for the country; if I tell them, I'm an islander they'd never know. I reckon they wouldn't have a clue who was an Aboriginal and who was an islander. We all look the same to them.'

'I think you're right, Fred, but why would you want to fight for a country that has rejected you? You can't vote, and you can't fight, all because of your race.'

'I still love Australia Elsie, and fighting for it might just change things. Not only that, I can earn six shillings a day. Just think how much I could return home with.'

'You've got to return home first. It's not going to be a picnic over there, Fred, thousands are dying.'

'I know, but I come from a long line of warriors; I have the instinct to survive. Don't you worry.'

'Yeah, famous last words. All right give it a go, you've got nothing to lose but your life.'

Fred fronted up to the recruitment office next day. His ploy worked without question; he was accepted into the Australian Imperial Force. He returned home to inform Elsie of his success. She was less enthusiastic than her husband.

Fred reported to the Cairns barracks where he was transported to Townsville for basic training.

He was assigned a hut, and upon entering the building he was surprised to discover the twenty recruits were all black – Torres Strait Islanders apparently. Most of them came from Western Australia and Queensland. The army hierarchy thought it would be best to keep all the blacks together so as not to upset the white recruits.

He introduced himself to those in the barracks and organised his kit. In the next bed to him was a fellow he knew from the docks; he too was a full blood from the same tribe. His name was Albert Spears.

'Well, what do you think, Bert? You ready to fight those Kraut bastards over there?'

'I reckon, Fred, mind you I've never met a fucking German, let alone killed one.'

'Don't worry, you can still shoot them having never met them.'

They both laughed.

'I wonder if they will keep us blacks together or mix us up with the whiteys?'

'Who knows, mate… we're just gunna have to wait and see.'

Alfred fitted in well and made new mates. Some were black and some were white. The standard training encompassed marching, polishing and marksmanship. Six weeks later the 51st was ordered to embark on the HMAT *Horata,* departing from Townsville and sailing to Alexandria in Egypt.

'Bloody hell mate, the biggest boat I've ever been on was a bark canoe except for the buggers we unloaded at the dock,' said Fred.

'Yeah, mate me too, it's going to be interesting.'

It certainly was interesting. Once the ship left the protection of the Great Barrier Reef the seas became extremely rough. *Horata* pitched and rolled, causing seasickness among most of the troops. None of the black soldiers suffered; they just took it in their stride.

Finally, they reached their destination, Alexandria, where they rested for a day and then marched in the searing heat to Mena Camp on the outskirts of Cairo.

The men enjoyed the usual tourist activities, including the pyramids and the Cairo nightlife.

The 51st's Mascot, Ken

39

Fred and Bert were amused by the reaction of the painted ladies in Cairo. Obviously, they had never seen an Aboriginal before and were quite intrigued by them.

Despite the temptation, the two Australian soldiers decided not to partake in the pleasures offered.

June 2, 1916

The 51st Battalion received orders to ship out to France; this news excited the men, but a fair amount of trepidation was also felt. This meant they would be marching into battle, not around the base of the great pyramid.

They boarded several troop ships. Fred and Bert's ship was named HMAT *Dunluce Castle.*

H.M.A.T "DUNLUCE CASTLE." 8,124 TONS.

The seas were much kinder on the Mediterranean than the Indian Ocean swells they endured on the voyage over. If they hadn't been heading over to fight a war, the trip would have been quite relaxing.

They disembarked in Marseilles and transferred to a train that would take them to Ypres where they camped among the ruins until they received their orders.

The word had filtered down to the troops that a fierce battle was taking place at a place called Pozieres. They soon saw ambulances and troop trucks loaded with the injured diggers.

'Bloody hell, Fred, it must have been some fight; these poor bastards certainly came out second best,' said Bert.

'Yeah, I hope we bloody march out rather than get a lift by ambulance.'

'Are you a bit nervous, mate?'

'Fucking oath mate, I wouldn't be human if I wasn't. We're about to face a whole lot of Germans who will do their best to kill us. Course I'm fucking nervous.'

Pozieres, a small village in the Somme Valley in France, was the scene of bitter and costly fighting for the 1st, 2nd, and 4th Australian Divisions in mid-1916.

The 1st Division on July 23, 1916 captured the village initially. The division clung to its gains despite almost continuous artillery fire and repeated German counter-attacks; the Australians suffered heavily. When it was relieved on July, 27, it had suffered 5,285 casualties.

The 2nd Division took over from the 1st and mounted two further attacks - the first, on July 29, was a costly failure; the second, on August 2, resulted in the seizure of further German positions beyond the village. Again, the Australians suffered heavily from retaliatory bombardments. They were relieved on 6 August, having suffered 6,848 casualties

Pozieres Trench After Battle

The 4th Division was next into the line at Pozieres. It too endured a massive artillery bombardment, and defeated a German counterattack on August 7; this was the last attempt by the Germans to retake the strategic village.

Moo Cow Farm

Chapter 6

Fred and Bert were resting along with the remainder of the battalion among the ruins of Pozieres. They found it hard to believe that Pozieres was once a picturesque village with tree-lined streets and cottages with neatly trimmed hedges. The scene was one of complete devastation. What were once cottages and buildings were piles of rubble impossible to identify.

Fred, Bert and Mates in Pozieres

Lieutenant Geoffrey Alcock, the officer in charge of the battalion, approached the Australian soldiers with new orders.

'Listen up men; we've been ordered to move down the road to a German stronghold. Apparently, they are bunkered down in a farmhouse; our orders are to attack and take it. It probably sounds straightforward enough, but our intelligence tells us there are hundreds of the bastards defending it.'

'Geez, it must be a fucking big farmhouse to hold all those Krauts,' Bert whispered.

'Either that or they've got a bloody big cellar.'

Mouquet Farm Cellars

Fred was unaware of just how right he was. The two soldiers and their battalion were about to embark on one of the most catastrophic battles Australian troops took part in during the war – The Battle of Mouquet Farm. The diggers called it either Moo Cow Farm or Mucky Farm, but whatever it was called, it was a killing field.

Moo Cow Farm was right in the middle of the Pozieres – Thiepval Ridge where the German Army had made its stand against the Allies. They had used it for eighteen months to establish strong defences.

The British Army had suffered shocking casualties in the Somme in early July 1916, assaulting the fortified machine guns and artillery head on as ordered by General Haig. On July 1st, in only one day, 20,000 died, and 40,000 were wounded; the worst day in British military history.

Three Australian Divisions were brought in from Belgium and entered the battle on July 23.

The buildings of the farm became a heavily fortified German stronghold. After much fighting around Pozieres, the Australian 4th Division gradually fought their way towards the farm on the August 7th. After fierce fighting, the 4thDivision, completely exhausted, was replaced by the 1st. Some gains were made at the cost of 92 officers and 2,558 men – virtually destroying the division. The 2nd. Division returned and in four days of fierce fighting lost 1,268 men and were again replaced by the 4th Division

The Australian forces were used seven times as a battering ram. On this one-mile

44

of the muddy front the Australian 1st, 2nd and 4th Divisions suffered 23,000 casualties between July 23rd and September 3rd, 1916.

Bert and Fred were together in the hastily dug trench; they had been enduring heavy artillery fire for the past eight hours, and it didn't seem like Jerry was going to let up anytime soon. The previous night they had been ordered by Lieutenant Alcock to creep forward through the thick slimy mud to try and establish a position closer to the farm. Six diggers followed them, bringing two Vickers machine guns, which they hoped would become a nest to attack the German positions.

Mouquet Farm Before and After Battle

'Private Spears and Barnes, I want you two to go over the top and make your way to that shell crater one hundred metres ahead. Once you have it secured, signal me and I will dispatch six other men with a couple of Vickers. We need to get closer to the German positions, or we'll be stuck here forever.'

'Yes sir, we'll do our best,' answered Fred.

The two diggers waited for the right time to go over the top.

'I bet you I know why Alcock wanted us to go, mate.'

'Yeah, why's that?'

'Because we're fucking black, mate.'

'What, you mean we're dispensable?'

'No, because the Germans won't see us in the dark.

'Yeah you're probably right, send the black diggers over and the Krauts won't know a thing until we're right on top of the bastards.'

There was a lull in the shelling, and now was the right time for them to move. They eased themselves over the top of the trench and started to slide through the thick mud. They couldn't go in a straight line as there were dead diggers everywhere.

After about an hour the two Anzacs reached the large shell crater. They rolled into it making sure the Germans didn't see them. Once settled in their new home they assessed the situation. The crater was certainly big enough to accommodate the two machine guns and their operators. The signal agreed upon was to fire three shots in the air, wait thirty seconds and fire three more.

Lieutenant Alcock would then send the gunner crews out into no man's land to undertake their perilous journey. The team of six was not as stealthy as the two Aboriginal soldiers. Lugging the Vickers made them even more vulnerable, the Germans saw them coming and opened fire, killing all six. Albert and Alfred were devastated as these young soldiers were their mates.

'Well, what in the fuck are we going to do now, Bert?'

'I reckon we should try to retrieve the guns, bring them back here and blast the fucking Krauts to smithereens. With luck, we'll get the bastards who got our blokes.'

'Do you know how to operate one of those things, mate?'

'Nope, but it can't be too hard. I'm sure we'll work it out.'

'Okay, let's do it.'

Bert and Fred, brothers in arms, clambered out of the crater and slithered their way across the killing field until they reached the dead soldiers. It was difficult for them both. They tried not to look at the mangled bodies with flesh torn off by German machine guns, but they couldn't help themselves.

'Don't worry boys, we'll get the bastards who did this,' whispered Fred.

They pulled the heavy machine guns through the mud and reached the crater without being detected by the German gunners.

The two diggers positioned the Vickers, ready to let the Germans have it.

'Hey, Fred, did you bring the ammo box with you?'

'No, I thought you had it.'

'Shit, we've only got one belt. That's no way near enough.'

'I'll go back and get it.'

'No mate, I'll go.'

'All right, we'll both go. It's probably fucking heavy anyway.'

Fred and Bert made the journey back. All the while there were artillery blasts and machine gunfire all around them. They retrieved the ammunition box and began crawling back, sliding the box behind them.

They pushed the heavy box into the crater and scrambled in after it. Fred felt a shooting pain in his right thigh; an enemy bullet had entered one side and exited the other. Bert used his medical kit to dress the wound and stop the flow of blood.

'Are you okay Fred? Just lie down and I'll get on with it.'

'Bullshit mate, I'm fine. I won't be able to run for a while, but I can still fire a bloody gun.'

'Fair enough, I'll load the ammunition belts, and we can have a bit of a go at these bastards.'

No Man's Land at the Farm

The two Aboriginal diggers fired their Vickers at the German positions, taking out two machine gun nests and restricting rifle fire from the enemy troops. Alcock took the opportunity to charge the German trenches with two hundred of his finest; they reached the enemy trench where hand-to-hand fighting raged for a full hour. The Australian diggers secured the trench. Lieutenant Alcock acknowledged the heroic efforts of Bert and Fred; he recommended they receive Military Medals for Bravery in the Field. They were presented to the two black soldiers three weeks later in Ypres.

The two heroic Aboriginal diggers moved on to see service on the Hindenburg line and took part in the ferocious battles at Messines and Polygon Wood in 1917.

On 25th April 1918, both Bert and Fred were involved in a counter-attack against the Germans at Villers-Bretonneux.

The Allied plan to recapture Villers-Bretonneux was simple but dangerous. The Germans had positioned a large number of soldiers and machine guns in the town. They were also placed along the railway embankment to the south and west. The enemy had also established themselves in the woods west of Villers-Bretonneux.

The commanders directing the attack were Brigadier–General William Glasgow, and Brigadier-General Harold 'Pompey' Elliot, two of Australia's best.

Their plan of attack was to initiate a night attack without a preliminary artillery bombardment. This would mean the Germans would not be pre- warned.

Two battalions, the 51st that Fred and Bert were attached to and the 52nd, 1500 men in all, were directed to attack the town from the south. The 13th would attack from the east.

Three more battalions, the 57th, 59th and 60th would attack from the north. This attack force amounted to about 2,400 men.

The objective was to encircle the Germans and trap them in the town where they would be annihilated.

Fred and Bert were advancing slowly along with the rest of their battalion. German machine guns located in the woods were hampering their progress and causing havoc amongst the troops. The 51st had suffered heavy casualties.

'Bert, we've got do something about those fucking machine guns or we won't be sipping beer in the village square tomorrow.'

'Yeah, I know. Do you reckon we can take them out?'

'We've done it before, so why not?'

'Fair enough. Let's go.'

The two Aboriginal warriors began to run as fast as they could, taking shelter behind the towering conifers. They eventually reached the point where they could be confident their grenades would land in the first German machine gun nest.

'Right Bert, let's give them hell.'

Both men pulled the pins on their grenades, waited a few seconds and hurled them. A massive explosion indicated they had found their mark.

'Beauty, now on to the next one,' said Fred.

The two diggers took out four more machine gun nests in the same manner. There was only one more to eliminate and then the battalion could move forward in relative safety.

'Okay Fred, this should be the last one, let's blow up the bugger and get back to the boys.'

Fred and Bert were creeping towards the machine gun nest when they both received a barrage of bullets in the back. The Germans had got wind of the attack and sent two of their best to take them out.

Both soldiers received their second Military Medals. Unfortunately, they would not be wearing them proudly on their dress uniforms.

They died on ANZAC day.

Lest We Forget.

Their country did forget.

The Tasmanian Devil

Chapter 7

A small, ferocious carnivorous marsupial, *Sarcophilus*, of Tasmania, having black fur with pale markings, strong jaws, and short legs: family *Dasyuridae Also called* **ursine dasyure.**

1914

Joseph Hanson lived in Ranelagh in the Huon Valley, Tasmania. His ancestral tribe, the Mellukerdee, had thrived in the valley for many thousands of years.

Aboriginal people had lived in Tasmania for at least thirty-five thousand years. Archaeological deposits have confirmed that the Aboriginal people in Tasmania survived the Last Glacial Maximum (LGM) around twenty-one thousand years ago At the end of the LGM around twelve thousand years ago, the sea level rose and Tasmania became isolated from the mainland of Australia.

Survival in this changing landscape was dependent upon the ability to harvest both aquatic resources, such as seals and shellfish, and terrestrial flora and fauna such as fern roots and wallabies, which Tasmanian Aboriginal people did skilfully, using the animal meat for food, bones for tools and skins as protective coverings or to build shelter. The Aboriginals developed watercraft, and a rich and dynamic culture continued despite the adverse climatic conditions.

In the early 1800s, Europeans colonised Tasmania and rapidly expanded onto Aboriginal land. Europeans and Aboriginal people began competing for the same resources, causing widespread conflict between the parties. Therefore, the government introduced policies to try to eliminate the "Aboriginal problem."

In 1829 the majority of the Aboriginal population were removed from the main island to a mission on Bruny Island under the direction of the Protector of Aborigines, George Augustus Robinson. The mission was a failure, due primarily to the effect of the introduced diseases such as pneumonia and tuberculosis. The mission was abandoned in its first year. Three further mission sites were subsequently trialled, including those on Flinders Island, and again, they all failed. Finally, in 1847, the surviving Aboriginal people were brought to Oyster Cove, to an abandoned convict penal station, where they were ignored and left alone.

Joe Hanson worked as a picker on the largest apple orchard in the area. It wasn't a well-paid job, but it was a job. Not many Aboriginals secured full-time employment in the valley, and Joe was grateful for the work at Grant & Sons. He was treated well and didn't suffer any racist treatment other than the odd 'where's your boomerang, mate', etc.

Joe watched the workforce diminish at Grant's as more and more eligible men enlisted. Even old Jim the foreman who was all of forty joined up. Mr Grant was finding it very difficult to replace them and as a consequence started to hire women to fill the vacancies.

Joe was becoming more and more anxious. He, as an Aboriginal, was barred from joining the forces even though he was probably fitter than most of the men who had gone over. He was regarded as the best boxer in Tasmania and had won many amateur belts over the past few years. His fighting name was "The Tassie Devil" and he lived up to the name.

While picking apples one clear day, his co-worker, John Healy, announced that he too had enlisted.

'Not another one. Soon I'll be the only one left,' said Joe.

'Well, why don't you join me, mate? We can discover the world together and shoot a few Krauts at the same time.'

'Mate, as if I didn't want to go. The problem is the bastards won't let me.'

'Why the fuck not?'

'Because I'm a bloody Aboriginal. They don't take black fellas.'

'That's bullshit, why?'

'I don't fucking know, all I know is if you're an Aboriginal you can't join.'

'Well, I've never heard of anything more ridiculous. Here they are crying out for men to join and fight for their country but they won't let able-bodied black men enlist.'

'Yeah, well that's the way it is. Nothing I can do to change it. You'll be climbing the fucking pyramids, and the Eiffel Tower and I'll be working with a whole lot of sheilas picking and packing apples.'

The next day John approached Joe with a plan.

'Hey Joe, I was speaking about you to my old man over dinner last night. He reckons he knows of a few Aboriginals who enlisted and are fighting overseas right now.'

'How'd they get in?'

'Well, he reckons you need to say you've got some white blood in you. Half-castes have been accepted, but not the full bloods.'

'But I'm a bloody full blood.'

'No, you're not. Your grandfather was a sealer, and he knocked up an Aboriginal girl.'

'That's bullshit, John.'

'Yeah, we know that, but the enlisting officer won't know it's bullshit. Joe, you spin them that story, and we can go over together.'

Joe went home that night and spoke with his father about John's plan on the veranda overlooking the Huon River. The house was very basic, but the veranda made it.

'So, you want to join up, Joe?'

'Yeah Dad, I do.'

'Why?'

'Well everybody I know has joined up, and I reckon seeing the world would be a good thing. Besides, they'll pay me six bob a day; that's got to be all right.'

'What I don't understand is this country won't let us vote or have a beer in a pub or own property. I'd love to buy this place, but the government won't let me. For God's sake we used to own the whole fucking country, and now they say I can't own this little plot. I'll be renting for the rest of my bloody life. And here's you, my only son, wanting to put his life on the line to protect Australia and some king halfway across the world.'

'Dad, I'm committed. I'm going, either way. I just want your blessing.'

'Okay, son, you have my blessing. Just keep your bloody head down and come back home when this bloody war is over.'

'Thanks, Dad I do appreciate it. They reckon it'll be over pretty soon anyway.'

'I hope so.'

Joe went into Huonville the following morning and entered the local recruitment office. There were about ten blokes in line and he was the only black. He was called up to the desk where two officers were seated.

'What's your name?'

'Joseph Parson, sir.'

'What's your address?'

'It's 190 Glen Huon Road, Glen Huon.'

'Nationality?

'Australian.'

'You're an Aboriginal are you not?

'Yes, sir, part Aboriginal and part Irish.'

'Irish hey, where did you get the Irish from?'

'My grandfather was an Irish sealer, sir.'

'All right, join that line for your medical.'

Joe naturally passed the medical and was officially a member of the Australian Imperial Force. He was to join the 15th Battalion and together with recruits from Queensland, he travelled to Victoria where they undertook basic training at Broadmeadows.

There were about ten indigenous recruits; seven from Queensland and the remainder from Tasmania. They were a mixture of half-castes, Maoris and Pacific Islanders, all proud Aborigines who were willing to lie so they could fight for their country and die if necessary.

Broadmeadows was horrible, a wet, muddy quagmire with disease rampant and morale low. What these recruits didn't know was these conditions stood them in good stead for what they were about to face.

The army collected the black recruits and housed them together so as not to upset the white recruits. As it turned out, they didn't receive any different treatment from the rest of the men. If they pulled their weight, they were accepted.

The usual basic training was endured and at the completion of six weeks the new soldiers were ready to go to war – well, that was the plan.

Joe and the 15th Battalion were transported via train to Albany, Western Australia, where they boarded the HMAT *Ceramic*.

The voyage was no different from any of the other troop voyages to Egypt. The soldiers endured rough seas, seasickness and boredom. Joe and John had become mates with some other diggers; Bill Rogers, an Aboriginal from Launceston, Rob Haley, from Hobart in Tasmania, and Keith Hodges from Townsville in Queensland. So, the gang of five comprised two black and three white men, all with one thing in common; they were soldiers in the Australian Imperial Force.

The 15th Battalion arrived in Alexandria and then moved to Mena camp where they were stationed for six weeks. Apart from the usual marching in exhausting heat and rifle practice, the boys partook in the delights of Cairo at night. There were no real incidents, although Keith decided he wouldn't be dying a virgin. He slipped away from the gang and found what he thought was a first-class house of ill repute.

The name of the establishment was "Arabian Nights" and the furnishings and the quality of the girls seemed excellent.

Keith sat down in a very luxurious room with big cushions and a large coffee table. A young scantily dressed girl offered him a coffee, which he accepted.

He was sipping his Arabian coffee when the madam entered the room, followed by six girls all wearing the same outfit as the young girl who brought him coffee.

'May I introduce you to my girls? All as you can see, are beautiful. You simply need to choose a number, and you will enjoy a wonderful experience you will never forget.'

Keith chose number three. She seemed a little older than the others and therefore would be more experienced.

She led him to a bedroom with a large bed draped in sheer linen so it looked similar to a four-poster.

'What is your name, soldier?'

'Keith. What's yours?'

'Babette.'

'Well, I'm pleased to meet you, Babette.'

'Well, Keith, how can I please you tonight?'

'To be perfectly honest I'm not sure. You see Babette, I'm a virgin.'

'Excellent, I'll teach you the art of lovemaking.'

'I wasn't much good at learning at school, but I can assure you I will be an excellent student, Babette.'

'The first step is undressing.'

Keith began to unbutton his uniform.

'No, no, my love that's my job; you just relax.'

Babette stood before him and proceeded to undress the nervous soldier, looking into his deep blue eyes the whole time. Finally, he stood there completely naked.

'I can see you are an excellent soldier, Keith.'

'What do you mean?'

'You are already standing to attention.'

They both laughed.

She then led the young digger to the bed and indicated he should lie down on his back. He did as he was told. Babette crawled up the bed and proceeded to perform fellatio. Keith had heard about this activity but couldn't imagine it felt this good.

The professional woman brought him to an explosive ending.

'That was fantastic, Babette, but I was hoping we would make love.'

'And so we will, darling that was just the first course.'

Over the next hour Keith, the virgin, became Keith, the lover. He thanked his teacher and returned to Mena camp determined not to divulge what had taken place that night – it was his secret.

Babette

The Gang of Five
Gallipoli

Chapter 8

April 9th, 1915

Bill walked into Joe and John's tent. They were both lying down on their stretchers resting after another day of marching in the Egyptian heat.

'Hey, have you heard the news? We're being shipped out tomorrow. Finally, we're going to see some action.'

'Great, it's about fucking time. I'm sick of this bloody sand and heat,' said Joe.

'Do you know where they're sending us to mate? I suppose it'll be France,' said John.

'The rumour is it won't be France. More likely Turkey.'

'Oh shit, I heard the Turks put up a bloody good fight at the Suez. Those bastards know how to fight.'

'Don't worry Johnno, we're up for it. Turks scream just as loud as Germans when they get stuck by a bayonet,' Joe said.

'Yeah, I suppose you're right. Anyway, it can't be any worse than being stuck here.'

The battalion was ordered to clean their rifles and sharpen their bayonets in preparation for the battle ahead. Not many of them slept well. Some wrote letters home to their wives, families, or sweethearts.

Reveille was at five am, they ate breakfast and then marched to the train station where they boarded a train bound for Alexandria. The four-hour trip was hot and cramped. The diggers were pleased to get off the bloody thing.

There were two troop ships for the battalion waiting at the dock; the HMAT *Seeang Bee* and the *Australind*. The gang of five boarded the *Australind*. It was dusk when they finally set sail, heading for Moudros on the island of Lemnos. This would be their staging point before landing at Gallipoli.

Moudros was only fifty miles from the Dardanelles where the Anzacs, British and French troops would launch their attack on the Ottoman Empire. The base was also a major hospital facility where light cases were treated initially. That status would change as the casualties from Gallipoli mounted.

Moudros Harbour 1915

Moudros Camp

The boys were allocated their tents and the waiting game commenced. They hoped that their stay at Moudros would be a short one, and they would be fighting the Turks very soon. Each day dragged. They were required to exercise and partake in rifle and bayonet practice as well as march, fucking march.

Two weeks passed then, just when they thought they would never get off the island, they received orders to assemble at dockside.

'Has anybody seen Keith?' asked John.

'No, come to think of I haven't seen him all day,' replied Bill.

'Well, he better get his skates on. We're meant to be on the dock in an hour.'

Their commanding officer approached the group.

'Are you lads ready to go?'

'Yes sir, only one problem; one of us has gone missing,' said Bill.

'What's his name?'

'Keith Hodges, sir.'

'It's okay; I know about him. He's been admitted to the field hospital. Unfortunately, he won't be joining us.'

'Did he have an accident or something, sir?' asked Rob.

'No, the silly bastard contracted V.D. when he was in Cairo. He reported to the medics this morning and he's going to be laid up here for the next few weeks.'

'Bloody hell, it's always the quiet ones. He never told us he got it off while we were there,' said Rob.

The four diggers marched down to the wharf and embarked onto the *Australind* where they were packed in like sardines. Although it wasn't quite summer yet, it was still bloody hot.

They set sail for Anzac Cove and an adventure they would never forget.

The 15th Battalion was assigned the role of follow-up; they would not be joining their Anzac comrades from the 9th, 10th, or 11th Brigades in the initial morning invasion. They would stay on the *Australind* and await the order to land at Anzac Cove.

The five Australian diggers watched from the *Australind* as the boats packed with Anzacs were towed to the shore carrying the Anzacs to an uncertain future. High Command was unsure to the level of defence the Turks would mount against the invasion.

The First Anzacs Being Towed to Gallipoli

It wasn't long before the Turks started to shell the cove. Shrapnel ripped into Anzac flesh and bullets were also doing their fair share of damage. The retaliatory shelling from the Allied armada made for a horrifying light show. Men were dying before they hit the sand, some drowning under the weight of their heavy packs while others were being ripped apart. Anzac Cove began to turn red.

'Fucking hell, those poor bastards don't have a chance,' said Joe.

'Don't worry Joe, they're Anzacs. We'll lose far too many that's for sure, but I bet we'll win the day,' Rob reassured his mate.

'I don't know about you blokes, but I count myself lucky we weren't in the first group,' said Bill.

'Do you reckon we'll be okay? I mean, those poor bastards have taken the worst of it. When we get ashore things may have quietened down,' said Johnno.

'I wouldn't bet on it, Johnno. I think we'll get a similar welcome,' said Joe.

'Do you blokes ever regret signing up?' asked Rob.

'Geez, we're just about to fight for the first fucking time, and you ask a stupid question like that,' said Joe.

'No, don't get me wrong, Joe. I am as committed as the next bloke.'

'Well, I suppose I get a bit narked when you white fellas starting questioning your reasons for joining. We black fellas had to lie and deceive just to get accepted.'

'What do you mean?'

'The Australian bloody Army banned Aboriginals from enlisting.'

'What for?'

'Because we're bloody Aboriginals, you know, black fellas, Abos, fringe dwellers.'

'So how in the fuck did you blokes get in?'

'We lied about our race; we either said we had white blood, or we were islanders. Bloody hell, Bill said he was a fucking Maori.'

'So why did you want to fight for a country that treats you like scum?' asked Rob.

'Well mate, I and the other blokes hope that by fighting for Australia our status will change, and we're given a fair go when we get back. Also, the money's much better than we could earn back home.'

'Fair enough. I hope you get what you want.'

'Things seem to be getting worse on the beach. The Turks certainly are not letting up,' said Bill.

Four o'clock came around, and the officers on board informed the nervous soldiers that they would be loaded onto the landing craft at 4 pm.

'Back home we used to have afternoon tea at four; I used to look forward to a nice cup of tea and one of Mum's homemade bickies,' said Bill.

'Well, you won't be getting tea and bickies today, mate. You'll be lucky to be eating beef jerky on the beach tonight,' said Rob.

The time came when they were ordered to assemble at the side of the ship where they would be required to climb down rope ladders and into the landing boats.

Anzac Troops Preparing to Board

Boarding Landing Craft

The officer in charge of the boarding was Lieutenant Bingham, a senior officer who had fought in the Second Boer War. He knew what these young men would face and couldn't help wondering how many would survive the landing.

It was time for Joe and his mates to climb the ladder down to the waiting landing boat.

'All right, men, down you go and keep your heads down. I'll see you on the beach,' Lieutenant Bingham reassured them.

One by one the soldiers climbed down into the small craft and took their seats. Joe was assigned an oar while the other four sat in the middle hoping they were in a safe spot, protected from bullet and shrapnel.

The steamboats towing them took off towards what would become known as Anzac Cove. The noise from the battlefield was deafening.

'Bloody hell, Johnno, this is all a bit scary. I hope we get to the beach alive,' said Bill.

'We'll be right, mate. Just keep your head low and listen out for bullets coming your way.'

'How the fuck will I know bullets are coming my way?'

'Don't worry son; you'll know.'

About four hundred yards from the beach, the steamers cut the rowing boats loose. Joe and the other oarsman began to row; they were now close enough for the Turkish machine gun bullets to reach them.

Bill had gone unusually quiet that was unusual for him.

'Hey Bill, are you all right mate?' asked Rob.

'Yeah, I'm okay. Just a little scared.'

'We all are, mate. Don't worry about that, fucking hell how could we not be?'

The boat neared the shore. Rob looked around at the rest of the diggers in the craft and couldn't believe that at least ten of the forty who started out on the short journey had been killed, and at least another five or six had severe wounds. He was so intent on his own safety he wasn't aware others had been hit. He was relieved that none of his mates had bought a bullet.

Lieutenant Bingham gave the order to disembark and run for the bottom of the cliffs where the first wave had established some sort of a beachhead.

Joe was the first to jump out. He disappeared under the water, which was about five feet deep. The weight of his pack made it tough for him to make his way. He finally found a footing and waded to the beach. Once on dry ground he ran as best he could with a wet uniform and a pack that weighed over forty pounds dry; God knows how heavy it was when wet. He safely made it to the cliff. Johnno, Bill, and Joe also made it. The same could not be said for the rest of the battalion, over one hundred men either died in the boats or on the beach cut down by Turkish bullets and shell.

The 15th were instructed to move to the left flank of the beachhead and then to move inland to support their comrades who had landed in the early morning. By the time they began to climb, night had descended over the bloody beach, bringing a dark curtain over the dead and wounded.

Lieutenant Bingham led his troops up the steep cliff face. The crumbling rock made it difficult to climb. The constant shellfire also contributed to the difficulty of the task.

'For fuck's sake Bill, this is getting a little ridiculous. Every time I take one step up I fucking slip back two. How in the hell are we going to make it to where ever the fuck we're supposed to be going?' complained Joe.

'Mate, we're all in the same fucking boat. Just keep going. There's no going back now.'

'Yeah well, I'd be a lot better off without these bloody wet boots; I'm an Aboriginal. I'm used to climbing in bare bloody feet.'

'I can't imagine you wandering around the Huon Valley in bare feet.'

'Yeah well, it's in me blood, forty thousand years of Australian bloody heritage.'

'Mate, the only blood you'll see tonight is your own if you don't shut up and keep going.'

Finally, the platoon made it to a valley, which would be later named "Shrapnel Gully" for good reason.

The Valley of Death

Chapter 9

The gully, leading into Monash Valley, became the main supply route of the Anzacs. The troops made their way through the valley and climbed the steep slopes to man the trench line along the second ridge at positions such as Quinn's Post and Pope's Hill. Transported up the gully went all the supplies essential to holding the line –food, water, engineering supplies and ammunition, while Turkish shells exploded overhead.

Supplies Being Moved in Shrapnel Gully

The men had no time to rest in the gully; their objective for the night was to reinforce the 10th and 11th Battalions in Monash Valley. Having discovered the Anzac trail, the Turks established several sniper sites. They were camouflaged and lethal, manned by their best sharpshooters.

'Right men, we need to keep going. Keep your eyes and ears open. There may be snipers above us,' said Lieutenant Bingham.

The lieutenant had hardly finished his words when a sniper's bullet struck him in the head. He collapsed onto the sandy soil, blood gushing from the wound. He was dead by the time he hit the ground.

'Fucking hell, quick— dive for cover everyone, there's bound to be more than one of the bastards,' yelled Sergeant Daley who was now in charge of the platoon.

The diggers lay prostrate on the harsh ground, hoping a sniper's bullet wouldn't select them next. Rob turned to his good mate and said, 'Dangerous place, mate.'

'Fucking oath it is, although I reckon I'm safer than you.'

'What do you mean by that, Joe?'

'I'm black. They can't see me. You, on the other hand, are pearly white, so you're an easy target.'

'I see your point mate. It's the first time I wished I was born black.'

'What do you mean?'

'Well, I've witnessed how the Australian Government treats you, blokes. I wouldn't wish that treatment on the Turks let alone my mates.'

'Oh, yeah, I see what you mean.'

Sergeant Daley gave the signal to move on. The Anzacs crept down the valley, ever vigilant ever watchful. Although snipers kept up their deadly attack, only one more digger was hit.

During the next few weeks, the 15th fought the Turks while at the same time digging a deep communications trench along Monash Valley. Sandbag walls were also constructed to give the men some protection from the Turkish snipers.

Joe had been identified by the 15th's replacement commander, Lieutenant Grace, as an excellent marksman. He was chosen to take on a counter sniper's role partnered by Rob who would act as his spotter using a telescope. The two soldiers would lie out all day observing Turkish sniper positions and firing on them when the least movement was seen. They became known as the best sniper team in the battalion and were respected by all the men including their commanding officer.

Despite all the precautions that were taken, Shrapnel Gully remained a very dangerous place.

Routinely each day a private with a donkey would ferry wounded soldiers from the battles taking place in the hills through Monash and Shrapnel Gully down to the medical clearing stations on the beach. He was a very friendly and jovial soul that seemed oblivious to the danger surrounding him. From April, 25th until May 19th he saved over three hundred wounded Anzacs.

It was on May 19th that Simpson was shot in the back by a Turkish machine gunner; he died instantly.

Simpson and His Donkey

Anzac Cove Clearing Station 02/05/1915

Joe immediately responded taking out the machine gun nest.

Private John Simpson Kirkpatrick was born in England in 1892 and was buried in Beach Cemetery Gallipoli.

He was recommended to receive the Victoria Cross posthumously, but the British Government denied this Australian request.

Beach Cemetery 1915

The 15th were charged with securing Pope's Hill and Quinn's Post.

Quinn's Post, named after Major Hugh Quinn, 15th Battalion (Queensland) AIF, was one of the most dangerous places on the Gallipoli peninsular. *'Men passing the fork in Monash Valley,'* wrote Charles Bean, *'used to glance at the place as a man looks at a haunted house.'*

Quinn's was positioned on the northern edge of the front line along Second Ridge, and just beyond was located Dead Man's Ridge, where Turkish snipers lurked, killing many Anzacs. Other Turkish trenches lay opposite; if the Turks could have advanced just a few yards more, Quinn's would have been captured, and the Anzacs annihilated.

The fighting at Quinn's between Turk and Anzac had been ferocious and unrelenting.

Joe and Rob took unprecedented risks every day in finding the right position to take out the Turkish snipers. The count by the middle of May was fifteen snipers although the toll the Turks had amassed was closer to one hundred Anzacs.

The other great threat to life and limb for both sides was hand grenades or bombs as they were called. There was a constant barrage of bombs thrown from either trench causing death and destruction to both sides.

'Hey, Bill we seem to be a bit low on bombs, mate. Can you move down to the beach and ask munitions for some more?' asked Johnno.

'Right-oh, mate. I'll see what I can muster up.'

'Keep your fucking head down cobber or you won't make it ten feet; the bastards are bad today.'

'Don't worry about me. I'll be back with the bombs before you know it.'

The bombs they both referred to were homemade explosives called jam tin bombs. The British had underestimated how many Mills bombs would be required for the campaign, so the Anzacs resorted to making their own. The jam tins were filled with gunpowder plus Turkish shrapnel and barbed wire. They were very rudimentary but effective.

The bomb factory was located on ANZAC Cove beach.

ANZAC Bomb Factory

Jam Tin Bombs

Bill arranged for two hundred bombs and three donkeys plus a private from 16th Battalion to escort him back.

The two soldiers were making their way through Shrapnel Gully when a shot rang out. Bill dropped to the stony ground blood pouring from his left eye. A sniper had shot him with uncanny precision. Now there were four.

Bill was a proud Australian soldier who fought and died for his country. He was also a proud Aboriginal who was forced to lie about his ethnicity just to have the right to become an Anzac. He wouldn't be going home to his beloved Tasmania and its magnificent forests where he had worked as a tree feller.

The soldier who had accompanied Bill, George Russell, continued the dangerous journey without mishap and arrived at Quinn's with his lethal cargo.

'Are you Johnno?' asked George.

'Yeah, that's me. What can I do for you?'

'I've got two hundred jam tins for you, mate.'

'Oh good, we can certainly do with them. It's been a bit of a one-way battle going on today. Where's Bill?'

'He copped one going through Shrapnel. I'm afraid he's dead mate, sorry.'

'Fucking hell no; not me good mate Billy. That stinks.'

'Yeah, I didn't know him, but he seemed like a good bloke.'

'He was, a bloody good bloke. Did they take him away for burial?'

'I don't know. I had to leave him where he fell.'

'Well, I'm going back to make sure he's looked after.'

The two Anzacs unloaded the bombs and when the task was completed Johnno approached his platoon leader to ask whether he could leave the line to find Billy and ensure he was buried at Beach Cemetery.

He was given permission to leave once the sun had gone down. He had two hours to wait before he could leave on his mission.

Jimmie's First Battle

Jimmie and Lou, along with their battalion, waited for the barrage to cease. When it finally did, they knew it was their time to go. Where? Over the top into no man's land, a place so inhospitable, so dangerous, that all soldiers, no matter how brave or courageous, dreaded taking their first steps onto this killing field.

The whistle blew, signalling to the first in line to climb the ladders and confront the deadly machine guns. Many of those young men fell before advancing one yard. Others disappeared, having been hit by artillery shells; their remains would never be found.

'For fuck's sake, this isn't what I signed up for; this is a massacre,' whispered Jimmie.

'We'll be all right. Just stick by my side, and we'll make those bastards sorry they ever took us on,' said Lou.

Captain Jones instructed the next group to climb over the top.

'That's us, Jimmie, remember to stick close by and keep your fucking head down.'

The two cobbers climbed the wooden ladder and headed towards the German trenches. Jimmie couldn't believe what he was seeing; there were dead Aussies everywhere. Some had fallen with no visible signs as to what caused their demise. Others had lost limbs while some were headless. He could hear the bullets whizzing by him, but none had hit their mark— not yet anyway. The smoke haze was so thick that he had trouble seeing two feet in front of him. He looked to his left to make sure Lou was with him; he wasn't.

Jimmie couldn't take the risk to find his mate. He just hoped he was okay. After what seemed an eternity but was in fact only twenty minutes, he stumbled across the German trench.

He rolled down into it, expecting Germans to be there to greet him, but it was empty. He looked out over the other side to see where the machine gun fire was coming from. What he observed was concrete bunkers two hundred yards forward.

'Fuck, that's all I fucking need. Another two hundred yards of no man's land before I get to stick a bloody Kraut,' he muttered to himself.

There were plenty of other diggers in the trench, all thinking the same thing. One of them was Captain Jones.

'Listen up men; intelligence has obviously got it wrong. Nothing we can do about that now, so we need to move on. I want you all to exit out of this God-forsaken trench and stay on your bellies. With any luck, the bastards won't see us coming in this smoke haze. Right then, let's go.'

The Australians began their assault as instructed; the machine gun fire hadn't abated but seemed to be going over their heads. Likewise, the artillery was blasting their trench line which was back a few hundred yards, allowing them to advance unhindered. Once the next German trench was in sight, Captain Jones ordered Jimmie and another digger, Robert Hill, to crawl as close as they could and throw several Mills bombs.

'You right mate?'

'Yeah, I suppose so, let's go,' said Jimmie.

The two soldiers slid their way forward until they could see the machine gun nest;

both pulled the pins and waited a few seconds. They didn't want the buggers to throw them back. They threw them together and both hit their mark; loud explosions blasted their eardrums– the guns fell silent.

The remainder of the platoon hurried forward and occupied the trench.

They waited for backup, but it never came. Eventually, Captain Jones ordered a retreat. The return journey was just as hazardous. The platoon lost a further ten men. Jimmie was struck by a piece of shrapnel but was able to return to his line for treatment. The black digger survived to fight another day. He was recommended to receive the Military Medal. High Command didn't approve it, but his comrade Robert Hill did receive the MM.

God Help Us

Chapter 10

Johnno and Rob were sitting on a ledge in the trench having a cup of tea and remembering their good mate Billy.

'We both should say a prayer for Bill,' said Rob.

'Yeah, I suppose you're right. You can say it, and I'll just bow my head.'

'Dear Lord, please look after Bill. He was a good man and an honest man and deserves to be with you in heaven. Amen.'

'Well that was short and sweet, mate, but nevertheless, I'm sure he'd appreciate it.'

'Yeah, as you know I'm not great with words. Being Aboriginal and all do you believe in Jesus?'

'Yeah, I was brought up a Catholic. I went to a Catholic school where they taught us ferocious natives all about Jesus and the Bible and that stuff.'

'What about the Dreamtime and the Song Lines, and other stuff you people believe?'

'Yeah, I believe in all that too.'

'With due respect, don't you think some mythical snake creating the rivers, valleys, and mountains is a little far-fetched?'

'Well, on the other hand, don't you think Jesus rising from the dead a bit hard to believe? The same bloke apparently walked on water, turned water into wine, and cured leprosy with the touch of his hand. To be honest doesn't that seem a little hard to believe?'

'Okay, I get your point.'

Joe joined them in the trench, not knowing what had happened to Bill. When he was told he was devastated. He bowed his head and sobbed.

The time came to go back down to Shrapnel Gully and get Bill organised in a proper grave. Joe volunteered to accompany Johnno to bury their Aboriginal brother.

They made their way into Monash Valley and then into Shrapnel Gully. There was a fair amount of shellfire and shrapnel flying around the place but the black

Anzacs made it without incident.

Once in Shrapnel, they looked around to see whether they could find an officer who could tell them where the day's casualties had been placed. Eventually, they found the fallen all laid out in neat rows. There must have been over a hundred men lying dead. It was a mournful sight.

Johnno was the one who discovered Billy. They asked the officer for permission to take their fallen brother down to the beach and bury him according to both Christian and Aboriginal tradition.

Permission was granted. The two men placed their mate on a stretcher and carried him down the rough steep path to ANZAC Cove. They discovered that burial plots had already been dug in anticipation of the day's casualties. Joe suggested a plot closest to the water. They placed Billy in the grave and said some words without mentioning his name. Then the two men performed a traditional chant and covered him over. A cross was placed at the foot of the grave with the simple words:

Bill Rogers

Born 1.1.1893.

Died 27.5.1915

Rest in Dreamtime.

Joe and Johnno made their way back to Quinn's, avoiding snipers and the odd shell. They were going to need a good night's rest as the morning would bring their most challenging day since they landed at Gallipoli.

May 28th 1915

The plan was to inundate the Turkish line with a barrage of bombs, forcing them to quit their trenches. Then the Anzacs would attack and capture and hold the enemy's line.

Each man was allocated several jam tins, which they would hurl upon Captain Little's command. The action was due to start at 6 am.

'How are you feeling Joe?' asked Rob.

'Pretty good mate. I'm looking forward to taking out some Turks for Bill.'

As they were waiting for the attack to begin a soldier approached them in the dark.

'G'day boys.'

'Well fuck me, it's Keith. What are you doing here?'

'Same as you I expect, I'm going to kill a few Turks.'

'Well, you took your time getting here, mate. No doubt you've been lying around in hospital getting your dick syringed by some sympathetic nurse. Meantime, we've been getting shot at with monotonous regularity,' complained Joe.

'Yeah, sorry about that. Didn't mean to let you down. I just picked the wrong whore I suppose.'

'Never mind, you're here now. It's good to see you, mate. The band of four is together again,' said Johnno.

'Four! What do you mean? We're five.'

'Sorry to tell you, but Bill's gone, he copped it yesterday,' said Rob.

'Bugger it, he was a good mate.'

'He surely was, to all of us.'

The time was approaching six and everybody in the Anzac trenches was on tenterhooks ready for the great assault. Captain Little checked his fob watch. With thirty seconds to go, he raised his whistle to signal the commencement of bombing. At precisely six he blew his whistle, fuses were lit and bombs were thrown. The Anzac's love of cricket paid dividends. Their accuracy was superb. Almost every bomb landed in the Turkish trenches.

At six thirty the order was given for the Anzacs to go over the top and run the few yards to the enemy line. Those Turks who survived the barrage were waiting to greet the charging diggers.

The fighting was ferocious; the sound of gunfire and the sight of bayonets from both sides ripping through flesh was horrifying.

Joe already had either shot or stuck several enemy soldiers. He was making his way to the far end of the trench where there seemed to be intensive fighting. As he clambered over a pile of dead bodies, he came face-to-face with a young Turkish soldier. They locked eyes.

Derya Oglu Yucel was seventeen years old. He was born and grew up in the beautiful coastal town of Bodrum, situated on the Aegean Sea. He was one of four brothers and three sisters. All the boys were soldiers fighting to defend Turkey from the invaders. Derya was a bright boy who excelled at school and was hoping to attend Constantinople University and qualify as a civil engineer after the war.

His dream was not to be; Joe stuck his bayonet through young Derya's throat and again into his chest. The young Turk fell to the bottom of the trench convulsing and then…nothing.

At the end of the day, the Anzacs had been successful in capturing the Turkish line. The enemy's survivors retreated, leaving over three hundred dead and wounded. The Anzacs also captured fifty Turkish soldiers.

The allies occupied these trenches for the next six months and although the Turks had made several attempts to recapture their ground the Anzacs held on.

The Turks were determined to rid their sacred soil of the invaders. They began a tunnelling project soon after losing their position.

The tunnel, when it was completed, ran for two hundred yards. The end of the tunnel was stacked with explosives destined to detonate directly under the Anzac trench.

When the day arrived most of the Anzacs were sleeping. The Turks detonated their bomb. The sound could be heard ten miles offshore by the British fleet steaming in with supplies and reinforcements for the Cove.

The devastation was enormous, and killed fifty-five Anzacs. The Turks confronted those diggers that survived with a major attack.

By noon that day, the Allied troops withdrew back to Shrapnel Gully. Included in the survivors was the band of four.

The 15th Battalion had been reduced to 600 men. They had lost 400 at Quinn's Post.

The decision was made by High Command to withdraw from Quinn's Post to enable the diggers to recuperate in a quiet sector known as "Rest Gully."

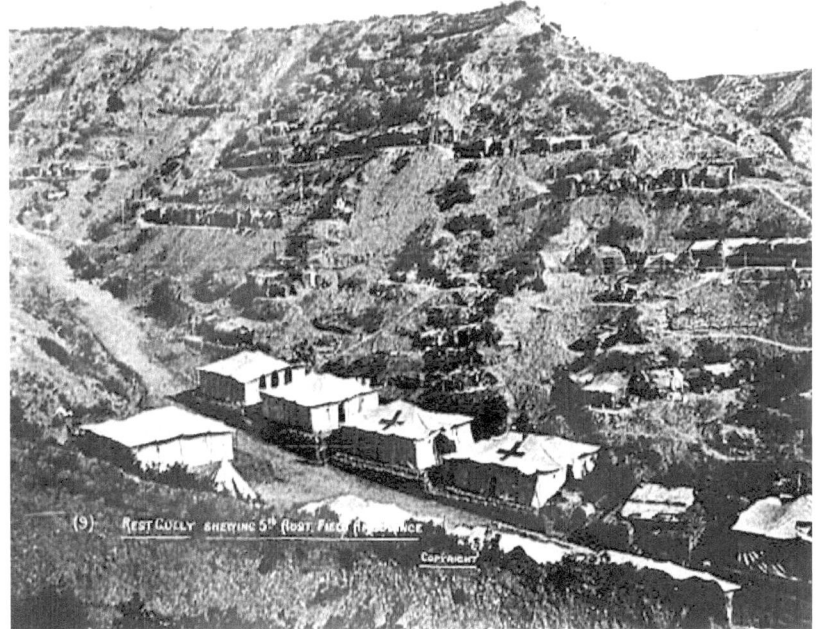

Rest Gully

'Well mate, this has got to be better than facing the fucking Turks across the paddock. I can't remember when I last used the bog without my 303 in hand,' said Johnno.

'Yeah, I can't agree with you more,' said Keith.

'You never did tell us whether you met any pretty young nurses while you were holed up in hospital.'

'Mate, having goo oozing from your dick and having a bloody big horrible syringe stuck up you each day is not conducive to courting a pretty young nurse.'

'No, I suppose not.'

'Nevertheless, there were a few nurses I would have liked to play mothers and fathers with.'

'I wonder how long they'll rest us here for?'

'Fucked if I know, but judging by the noise of battle in the distance it won't be too bloody long.'

'It's a shame we don't have Bill here with us...'

'Yeah.'

'Did you know he was a painter?'

'No, what did he paint?'

'Mainly landscapes, but sometimes he'd paint a portrait of an elder or a young kid. He didn't sell any though; Aboriginal paintings aren't in demand but lots of his people own a Bill Rogers painting.'

'How come Aboriginal paintings aren't in demand? I would have thought if the painting was good it didn't matter who painted it.'

'Keith, you have a lot to learn mate, our people are excluded from pretty well everything. I mean you think about it we can't vote, we can't drink and we can't even join up to fight for our country. We don't even know how many there is of us. We're not included in the census; they don't even register our births.'

'It's bloody crazy, mate; I hope we can change things when we return home.'

'I wouldn't bet on it, Keith but where's there's hope…'

The 15th Battalion stayed on at Rest Gully for two months during that time. Some five hundred reinforcements joined them.

Now they were at full strength, they had a job to do.

August in Turkey
You Wouldn't Want to be Here

Chapter 11

August 6 1915

Continued failure to advance the frontline formed at Helles forced General Hamilton to formulate a new approach to taking the higher ground at the Gallipoli Peninsula. His focus now turned to capturing the Sari Bair ridge.

His plan was for two new British infantry divisions to land at Suvla Bay while Anzac troops mounted an offensive on both Hill 971 and Chunuk Bair on the morning of August 7, and met up with the British, north of Sari Bair. An attack on the Nek by the 3rd Australian Light Horse was planned to coincide with the New Zealanders taking Chunuk Bair to surround Baby 700 from both sides. The objectives of the Suvla Bay landing was the capture of the ridges to the north, called Kiretchtepe and east, Tekketepe, and a line of hills to the south on The Anafarta Spur.

Baby 700

As a diversion, on August 6, the Anzacs successfully attacked and captured a Turkish trench at Loan Pine. This resulted in some of the bloodiest fighting in the entire campaign. A simultaneous British attack at Krithia Vineyard in the

Helles sector, however, was not successful and was again marked by the heavy casualties that characterised all battles in the area.

The Ottomans were only partly deceived by these feints and sent heavy reinforcements to the north on August 7 where they encountered the New Zealand Infantry Brigade marching on Chunuk Bair and prevented their capture of the summit until the following morning. This delay was to cost the Light Horse dearly at the Nek.

August 7 1915

The Nek is remembered for the futile tragedy it was, the charge of the Australian Light Horse Brigade and the irresponsible so-called leadership, which were responsible for so many young men's lives lost.

The original plan had envisaged the New Zealanders attaining Chunuk Bair and then coming down the range behind the Turkish positions to the Nek. However, this did not happen. Just before dawn, the lead New Zealand battalion–the Otagos–were still short of Chunuk Bair. General Birdwood, the commanding officer of the Anzac forces, allowed the light horsemen to proceed in order to give all possible support to the Chunuk Bair assault. If Turkish reinforcements could be held from that vital height for even an extra half hour then its capture, the main purpose of the August offensive, might well be achieved. However, Birdwood had written earlier of the Turkish positions at the Nek and up the slopes of Baby 700:

> *These trenches and convergences of communication trenches ... require considerable strength to force. The narrow Nek to be crossed ... makes an unaided attack in that direction almost hopeless.'*

At 4.30 am the first wave of the 8th Light Horse Regiment, men from Western Victoria, rose from their trenches and dashed for the Turkish line at the Nek. Minutes later a second wave went over. Lieutenant William Cameron, of the 9th Light Horse, was watching the charge:

> *We saw them climb out and move forward about ten yards and lie flat. The second line did likewise ... As they rose to charge, the Turkish Machine Guns just poured out lead and our fellows went down like corn before a scythe. The distance to the enemy trench was less than 50 yards, yet not one of those two lines got near it'.*

The Charge at the Nek

Within half an hour two further waves, men of the 10th Light Horse from Western Australia, met a fate similar to the Victorians'. From his vantage point on the approaches to Chunuk Bair to the north, Sergeant John Wilder of the Wellington Mounted Rifles saw the destruction of the 8th and 10th Light Horse:

> *'I saw the whole thing ... and don't want to see another sight like it. They were fairly mown down by machine guns.'*

Probably the attack on the Nek achieved its purpose of holding temporarily near Baby 700 at least part of the Turkish reinforcements that were just then streaming northward towards Chunuk Bair.

The charge at the Nek was the most senseless and tragic waste of Australian lives at Gallipoli.

The hundred and forty Australian lives were wasted by two incompetent Australian officers, Brigadier General Frederick Hughes and Lieutenant Colonel John Antill.

The Aftermath of the Charge at The Nek

The Nek – Many didn't make it out of the Trench

General Hughes

Colonel John Antill

The New Zealand forces at Chunuk Bair also suffered terribly, as casualties of 711 of the 760 who held the peak two days before being relieved by two British battalions. The battalions were subsequently evicted by an Ottoman attack led by Mustafa Kemal, the future president of modern Turkey.

Meanwhile, troops led by John Monash and an Indian brigade became lost on the way to the Hill 971 objective.

Although the beaches were only lightly defended, the Suvla landing echoed the Anzac landing in its confusion. Little ground was gained in first two days, despite enormous casualties. On the morning of August 9th, Turkish reinforcements forced back the attack, and fighting continued until the final British offensive on August 21 at Scimitar Hill and Hill 60.

Successful capture of these points would have united the Anzac and Suvla fronts, but that was not achieved, and the August offensive drew to a halt.

Let's Get Out of Here

Chapter 12

Rob, Keith and a few mates were resting after their unsuccessful push to take Abdel Rahman Bair otherwise known as Hill 971.

Johnno and Joe joined them.

'Well that wasn't much fun was it?'

'No, we achieved nothing Rob; fuck all, in fact,' responded Keith.

'I really do wonder why we're here at all. It's obvious the Turks aren't too happy having us visit their lovely country,' said Joe.

'I reckon our time's nearly up; for God's sake, we can't keep throwing ourselves at Turkish machine guns. Did you hear what happened at the Nek?'

'Yeah, fucking disgusting. Hughes and Antill should be publicly horsewhipped.'

The Anzacs would get their wish; the evacuation was being planned as they spoke.

Churchill's Gallipoli campaign was becoming more and more unpopular in Britain and its allied countries, including Australia and New Zealand. The casualty numbers and the ever-growing list of failures were making the campaign harder and harder to justify. The need for men and resources on the Western Front was becoming more acute. Gallipoli was going nowhere and it was clear that the British had seriously underestimated the fighting spirit of the Turks.

General Monro

In October 1916, General Sir Charles Monro replaced General Hamilton. He proposed an evacuation of the troops in Gallipoli. The weather faced by Allies in the next few months tore at the troops with flooding followed by snow killing many soldiers from exposure or drowning in the trenches, leaving both sides feeling miserable.

Winter Wonderland at Gallipoli

Finally, the war council agreed to evacuate the troops still posted on the Gallipoli Peninsula, having accepted Lord Kitchener's recommendation.

The self-firing rifle used for the evacuation of Gallipoli

In contrast to the landing, the evacuation took place without the Turks realising that the Allies were leaving. Soldiers rigged self-firing rifles in the trenches and along the front line to trick Turkish soldiers into thinking there were still Anzacs fighting.

'Come on Keith, it's our turn to go. You don't want to miss the boat,' said Rob.

'You carry on, mate. I'm staying put for a while. After all I'm due to make up for a bit of time I missed at the start.'

'What in the fuck are you talking about? We're all leaving, mate, right now.'

'Nope, not me. I volunteered to stay on with Colonel Paton. We're going to keep firing our 303s and keep the water up in the self-firing rifles to fool the Turks. We're on the last boat to leave this Godforsaken shore.'

'Right, I'm staying too,' said Rob.

'We're staying as well,' said Joe and Johnno.

'Bullshit fellas, fuck off on the boat. I'll see you on the ship. Besides, there's not enough room on our boat for another three. Not only that, but Paton has got to approve you.'

The three Anzacs reluctantly agreed and made their way to the pier where the boats were waiting to ferry them to the *Australind*, the same ship that brought them to the peninsula.

Joe and the Lads Waiting on the Beach

The Anzacs placed a huge mine in no man's land and when it was detonated the Turks thought they were facing a major attack. They opened fire with machine guns and rifles in a barrage which lasted nearly an hour.

By the time Turkish troops realized they had been fooled it was too late. The New Zealand troops left Anzac Cove and Suvla on December 19 and 20, with the last British soldiers evacuated on the nights of January 8 and 9.

Gallipoli Goodbye

Evacuation by Raft

Anzac soldier placing flowers on graves for the unknown dead

When the allies sailed back to Egypt, they left behind thousands of their dead comrades on the shore. It wasn't easy for them to leave. Many felt guilty, angry, and frustrated to abandon their dead comrades in defeat, but they also recognized it was hopeless to continue the campaign. Nobody felt the grief more than Joe, Rob, Johnno, and Keith for their good mate Bill.

They would soon discover the Western Front would be no easier than Gallipoli, and maybe worse.

Back in the Land of the Pharaohs

Chapter 13

The *Australind* docked at Alexandria on the morning of Christmas Eve 1915; once all the troops disembarked they marched to Central Station and boarded the train to take them to Cairo and Mena Camp. It was just like coming home for the battle-weary Anzacs.

That evening once the boys had settled into the tent city they gathered together to sing Christmas carols. They all held candles so they could follow the song sheet.

The rest period didn't last long. On the 27th training began and although the lads resented being trained, it was a holiday compared to what they endured at Gallipoli. Training encompassed marching across the desert in full pack. This was what they had to do prior to leaving for Gallipoli; most felt it was a complete waste of time.

They did have recreation breaks where they would play cricket; Australia versus New Zealand.

The score:

New Zealand 9 for 186

Australia 10 for 184

The Australians were not impressed.

Joe and Rob were sitting on their stretchers in their tent when Johnno came in with a grin from ear to ear.

'What are you looking so happy about? You look as if you've received your orders to return home,' said Rob.

'I fucking wish… No, I've just had a conversation with John McKay, you know, the Kiwi batsman that killed us today.'

'Oh yeah, what did he want— a rematch?' asked Joe.

'No, he asked whether we would like to challenge their bloke in a boxing match.'

'Yeah, how much are they willing to put up for the purse?' asked Joe.

'Wait for it, one hundred quid!'

'Bullshit; no way.'

'Yeah, that's what I said, but he assures me he's fair dinkum.'

'What do you reckon Joe, are you up for it?' asked Johnno.

'That depends, who are they putting up?'

'Some bloke called Ernie Abbott. Do you know him?'

'I don't know him, but I've heard of him. He's bloody good; he won the New Zealand amateur title in 1913.'

'Come on Joe you're the Tassie Devil, you've only ever lost one fight.'

'Yeah, it could be two pretty damn soon.'

'Joe, we'll back you, mate. We'll all help you train,' said Johnno.

'I used to be a pretty handy boxer mate. I'll be your sparring partner,' said Rob.

'When do they want to fight?' asked Joe.

'In four weeks,' said Johnno.

'It doesn't give me much time to get fighting fit.'

'Have a think about it, Joe. I said I'd get back to him with an answer tomorrow.'

'Okay, I'll think about it tonight.'

Next morning the three mates approached Joe.

'Morning Joe, did you sleep well?' asked Johnno.

'Not really. I'm still not sure. I don't want to let you blokes down.'

'You won't be letting us down mate, win, lose or draw. If you don't feel comfortable about fighting we fully understand,' said Rob.

'Well, here's the condition. If I win, we split the prize money.'

'No, it's your prize mate, not ours,' said Keith.

'Then, I don't fight.'

'So, if we agree to the split, you'll take this bastard on?' asked Keith.

'Yep, that's the deal.'

'What do you reckon, fellas?'

'Okay, if that's what Joe wants,' said Rob.

The others agreed; Joe would fight for a purse for the first time in his boxing career.

For the next four weeks, Joe trained in his spare time, sparring with Rob who turned out to be a more than adequate sparring partner.

Finally, the day of the fight came and more than two hundred Australian and New Zealanders jostled for a good possie to view the fight. Although betting was illegal many of them placed a bet with the SP bookie, an Australian corporal.

Joe was the first to enter the ring with his trainer Rob in the corner holding the white towel – the towel he hoped he wouldn't need to throw into the ring.

A roar went up from the Australian diggers; they began the chant 'Tassie Devil'.

Ernie then joined him and immediately performed the traditional Maori war dance, the Haka. Joe stayed in his corner giving his opponent the respect he was due.

The referee for the match was Lieutenant Colonel Harry Smith from the Australian 16th Battalion. He was a Rhodes scholar and a formidable boxer in his day. He would determine the winner on points unless a knockout occurred.

Round One

The two fighters tentatively approached each other, circling the ring like cats. Ernie threw the first punch, which Joe evaded, responding with a body punch to the ribs. The punch clearly hurt Ernie, and the rest of the round was purely sparring.

The following nine rounds were evenly balanced with points being distributed on an equal basis.

The final round bell rang and the two tired fighters faced each in the centre of the ring. Both of them knew this was the round they must win.

Ernie threw the first punch, hitting Joe on the left jaw. His head was thrown back, and sweat sprayed out, hitting the ringside supporters. Joe swayed on his feet and Ernie, sensing the kill, went for the knockout blow. Joe still had enough savvy to see the punch, so he ducked, and with all the strength remaining in his body hit Ernie with a massive uppercut to the chin. Ernie dropped to his knees and then collapsed on the canvas.

Lieutenant Colonel Harry Smith began the count. At the count of eight Ernie lifted his head from the canvas but dropped it back down. He was done.

The chant went up for the Tassie Devil. Joe was the champion.

Harry Smith was the custodian of the purse. He approached Rob after the bout, presenting him with Joe's prize money, one hundred pounds.

Joe scrubbed up under the canvas shower the troops used at Mena and then went and met his mates at the canteen.

'Here he is, the undisputed champion of Australia. How are you feeling, champ?' asked Johnno.

'A bit sore and weary to be honest, mate, but I'll be all right.'

'You were magnificent, Joe. We're all proud of you; not just us, but the entire Australian Imperial Army,' said Keith.

'Well I'll tell you what; I wasn't far from going down. I just came up with a lucky punch at the right time.'

'Don't underestimate your achievement, Joe, you're a champion,' said Rob.

'Thanks, mate, I appreciate your support, particularly you, Rob leading up to the fight and being in my corner.'

'It was my honour, mate. Now, we need to divvy up the spoils of your labour.'

Rob took the prize money from his trouser pocket and divided it four ways. Joe had decided to keep ten pounds and send the remainder to his mother and father back home in Tasmania.

What he didn't know was his three cobbers had decided to do the same. Joe's folks would receive sixty pounds; a sizable amount.

The next day they received their orders; they would travel to Alexandria and then sail to France. Their war would become even more intense.

C'est parti pour la France on y va.
It's Off to France We Go

Chapter 14

Embarking at Alexandria, Egypt

Once boarded on the troop ship *Themistocles* they settled in and discovered this ship was by far and away the most comfortable vessel they had sailed on thus far.

The ship set sail that evening. The usual precautions against fire and submarines were dutifully observed. Life belts were issued, and lifeboat stations practised daily. At night, the ship observed a complete blackout. Unlike their voyage from Australia, the weather proved to be ideal.

'Well mate, if this is an indication of what's ahead; Viva la France. I haven't felt this good since leaving home,' said Joe.

'Don't get to carried away Joe; this is only the beginning and who knows what really lies ahead of us. Having said that, this is a bloody good ship,' said Rob.

A new training regime was adopted on the promenade. Emphasis was given to the correct use of a gas mask and what to expect in the trenches of France and Belgium. The boys agreed by the sounds of it that there wasn't much difference to the trenches in Gallipoli.

Sunday, March 19th

'Hey Keith, have you got any idea why we seem to be zig zagging?'

'Buggered if I know Johnno, it could be to avoid a U-boat or something.'

'Fuck, I hope not, I'm not keen to go for a swim right now.'

'I know what you mean; I hate the fact you can't see the buggers. At least with a battleship you can see where it is and when it opens fire.'

They were fortunate; the *Themistocles* sailed on without harm. Later in the day, they heard a troop ship had been torpedoed not far from where they were sailing.

The ship sailed on to Crete, passing the north side during the early evening of the same day, and later the next day they arrived off Malta.

The troops caught a glimpse of the harbour with its narrow entrance and heavy fortifications.

The men could see the naval ships leaving the harbour. There were both French and British destroyers, plus a submarine.

The *Themistocles* continued on her course through the Malta Channel and into the Sicilian Sea. The course took them onto Sardinia and Corsica, and finally, they sighted the French town of Toulon and the great French naval base.

'Well lads, it won't be long now before we dock at Marseilles,' said Rob.

'I suppose we're not going to get a chance to do some sightseeing. I've heard Marseilles is a beautiful ancient city,' said Joe.

'Not what we're here for I'm afraid, Joe. I reckon we'll dock and get straight onto a train up north,' said Keith.

'Hey, fellas what do you think that bloke on the little boat's all about? He's yelling something through his megaphone,' said Johnno.

'Yeah and the bloke on the bow is waving his bloody arms furiously,' said Joe.

What all the panic was about was that the ship was heading straight for a minefield. The captain had not been informed, and the field was certainly not charted. The ship changed course and finally entered the harbour.

A band was waiting and began playing *Marseillaise*. There was a small crowd waiting to welcome the new Australian arrivals, waving flags and yelling *Viva la Australie*.

The diggers' sea journey had come to an end.

The Western Front awaited them.

The four cobbers were loaded onto a steam train taking them to Poperinge in Belgium. The journey lasted two days and most of the time was taken up with playing cards and writing home to their families and sweethearts.

Railway Depot, Poperinge

'Geez mate it's a busy place. Bloody soldiers everywhere,' said Joe.

'Yeah, it makes you wonder if there's any soldiers left fighting on the front. They're all here getting pissed and shagging the local girls in Poperinge,' replied Johnno.

'Mind you, that sounds all right to me,' said Joe.

The officer in charge of the battalion was Lieutenant Colonel Williams. He ordered the troops to march through the town to the tent city where they would rest and take leave for two days before moving forward to the front.

'Fucking hell, I thought the train station was busy but it has nothing on this,' said Rob.

CAMPAGNE DE 1914   POPERINGHE — Artillerie Anglaise sur la Grand'Place

I suppose all these artillery wagons are heading for the same place we are,' said Joe

'Yeah I think you're right, mate,' said Rob.

'Once we're settled into our new digs I reckon we should go exploring. From what I hear this is the place to spend my ten quid,' said Joe.

They all agreed, and the spring in their marching step was obvious. They were all going to have a bloody good night.

They reached the tent city which would be home for the next few days.

'I don't know about you blokes, but I'm gunna find the showers and clean up before I adventure into town tonight,' said Rob.

'I'm with you mate. We have to pass the short arm inspection when we get to La Lanterne Rouge,' said Keith, laughing.

'You seem pretty blasé for someone who picked up a dose in Cairo.'

'I'm prepared for all events this time. I've got a supply of Englishmen's overcoats as they call frangers in this part of the world.'

'Where did you get those?' asked Joe.

'When I was being treated in hospital one of the nurses handed me a dozen, telling me to wise up and use them in the future.'

'Well mate, you better hand them out. I think we're all gunna need the little fellas.'

'By the way, where did you hear about La Lanterne Rouge, Keith? Don't tell me it was the same nurse who gave you the frangers?' asked Johnno.

'No, don't be stupid. I was talking to a bloke on the ship. He got a letter from his older brother who's been here a while. He reckons the Red Lantern is the best in Pops.'

'Fair enough, sounds good enough for me.'

The four expectant diggers ate dinner in the mess hall and headed off to discover the delights of Poperinge.

It didn't take long for the intrepid Aussies to discover the red light district. There were soldiers from all the allied nations walking the streets looking for the best establishment where they could spend their hard earned money.

La Lanterne Rouge stood out from the others with its red lantern hanging over the red door. Rob, being the eldest, decided he would lead the group into the reception room where a stunning mature woman was sitting at a desk playing some sort of dice game.

She welcomed them in and introduced herself as Madame Charlene.

'So boys, you would like some passion tonight?'

'Yes Madam, we've just arrived from fighting in Turkey and we're heading off to the front in a few days. We all could do with some passion as you say,' explained Rob.

'No problem, you will like my girls. Who are these beautiful black men? We do not see many in Poperinge.'

'We're Aboriginals from Australia,' said Joe.

'My girls will love you both, black men are very popular although as I say, uncommon.'

'So Madam, how much do you charge for an hour?' asked Rob.

'Five francs, monsieur.'

'Do you mind if I speak with my mates before committing, Madam?'

'Of course *chéri*, but don't take too long or you may miss out.'

Rob got the group together and explained the price. They all agreed it was a lot of money; however, it would be worth it.

'Madam, we would all like to take one hour with one of your beautiful girls,' said Rob.

'One girl, four men that's unusual – however…'

'No, you misunderstand, Madam; we would all like a girl each for one hour.'

'Oh, that sounds more practical. That will be twenty francs in total.'

The boys paid their money over to Madam Charlene who led them into a very opulent lounge where they could choose the lady they wished to spend time with.

The four boys were completely gobsmacked; they just stood there staring at the half-naked ladies not able to utter a word.

Madame Charlene was used to this reaction, and she got things moving by introducing each of the ladies by name.

Eventually, each digger made his choice and was shown into a private bedroom. Here they stayed for a full hour.

Out of the four diggers, three entered the boudoir as virgins. Only Keith had some experience, albeit painful.

They met outside in the street and compared notes.

'How fucking good was that?' asked Rob.

'Fucking good in every sense of the word,' said Joe.

'Well, I don't know about you blokes but I'm back again tomorrow night,' said Johnno.

They all agreed; they would return the next night, their last in Pops.

The Western Front was their next port of call.

It's Not a Giant it's a Windmill
Don Quixote

Chapter 15

The four Aussie soldiers were feeling on top of the world. Their lustful time in Poperinge had lifted their spirits and given them a new incentive to live a little longer.

They were going to need all the key elements to survive the next year or two; bravery, luck, and competent commanders.

They boarded the train at the railway terminus and headed for Albert where they would commence their march to the once pretty village of Pozieres just down the road. The battalion spent an uneasy night in Albert. The Germans were shelling the town constantly and the British retaliated in kind. The noise of the artillery didn't make for a good night's sleep.

Reveille sounded at six the next morning. A magnificent breakfast of bully beef, biscuits and tea was consumed before they assembled for the march to Pozieres. The order was given, and the 15th Battalion and the rest of the Australian First Division, fifteen thousand men in all, began their journey down the Albert – Bapaume Road.

The troops sang various marching songs including Waltzing Matilda, Click Go the Shears and It's a Long Way to Tipperary.

The singing lifted the men's spirits as they got closer and closer to the battlefield.

At last, they reached Command Headquarters; if a couple of dugouts could be described as HQ.

The officer commanding the 1st, 2nd, and 3rd Battalions was Captain William Bannister, a solicitor back in Australia and regarded as a fine commander and soldier. His orders from Major General Walker were to make his troops ready for an attack within twenty-four hours. Walker's orders in turn came from General Gough. Major Walker argued that the 1st Division had just arrived at the front having marched from Albert. His argument was based on the fact the men were exhausted and would put up a better fight if they were rested. General Gough, known for his gung-ho approach, insisted on attacking the following night. The recipe for slaughter had begun; a recipe Gough would follow throughout the war.

The attack was launched on July 23 1916. It was to become known as the Battle of Pozieres Ridge. Australian and British forces fought hard for an area that comprised a relatively high observation post over the surrounding countryside. There was also the additional benefit of offering an alternative approach to the rear of the Thiepval defences where the Germans were entrenched.

The Australian 1st Division Anzac Corps, having served in Gallipoli, was primarily given the task of capturing Pozieres Ridge. This had been an objective for capture on the first day of the Somme Offensive; an objective that was never realised. The Australians succeeded in capturing the ridge by August 4th, having launched their offensive almost two weeks earlier. The British 48th Division assisted them in the attack.

Once the Australian diggers succeeded in capturing Pozieres village itself, they moved across the main road towards "Gibraltar," a German strongpoint. A mere two hundred yards separated the Australians from Pozieres Ridge, the attack's main objective. It was heavily defended by the securely entrenched German troops. Two lines of trenches needed to be overcome before the ridge could be claimed. This action created a heavy toll on the Australian and British troops; the Germans didn't fare much better.

Later on that first day, July 23rd, the British 17th Warwickshire Regiment joined the Australians to the northwest of Pozieres village. The Germans weren't going anywhere; they defended the ridge valiantly.

The 2nd Australian Division subsequently relieved their comrades and continued the attack on the ridge for a further four days before they too were relieved. Allied casualties at this stage were running at a costly 3500.

The ridge finally fell after almost two weeks of bitter fighting on August 4th. However, both Mouquet Farm and Thiepval remained under German control.

Despite the intensity of the fighting at Pozieres, the four diggers remained unscathed although they were utterly exhausted.

'I don't know about you blokes, but I'm hoping like hell the bastards give us a rest,' said Joe.

'You mean the Germans, mate?' asked Johnno.

'No, I mean Gough and his toffee-nosed mates up at High Command.'

'Well, after what we've just gone through, I'm sure they'll give us a spell to recuperate a little,' Keith said.

'Not fucking likely. I bet they're already typing out the orders for our next push,' said Rob.

He was right. General Gough was keen to attack the next German-held position, Mouquet Farm, only a few kilometres from Pozieres.

Imagine a gigantic ash heap, a place where dust, and rubbish have been cast for years outside some dry, derelict, God-forsaken up-country township. Imagine some broken-down creek bed in the driest of our dry central Australian districts, abandoned for a generation to the goats, in which the hens have been scratching as long as men can remember. Then take away the hens and the goats and all traces of any living or moving thing. You must not even leave a spider. Put here, in evidence of some old tumbled roof, a few roof beams and tiles sticking edgeways from the ground, and the low faded ochre stump of the windmill peeping over the top of the hill, and there you have Pozières.

CEW *Bean*, Letters from France, Melbourne, 1917, pp.113–4

Colonel Jack Parsons approached the battle-fatigued soldiers of the 15th with the news they were to assemble and begin their march to the farm. Rob looked at the other three and said, 'I told you so.'

It wasn't a sprightly enthusiastic group of men heading down the road, passing bloated bodies, both Australian and German, together with countless dead mutilated horses and the odd dog. Nothing much escaped that horrible battle.

Pozieres to Mouquet Farm Road

The Pozieres-Thiepval road leading to the farm was exposed to the German artillery positions. They took full advantage, raining shells down on the advancing Anzac troops.

'Fucking hell these bastards mean business, Joe, keep your head down or you'll fucking lose it,' screamed Rob.

'You don't have to tell me, mate, my head's so far down it's almost up my arse.'

'Where's Johnno and Keith? They were right behind us before the Krauts started hammering us,' Rob said.

'Shit, I don't know, but we can't move back or we'll be dead. I'm sure they're okay. You wait, as soon as we start moving again Johnno will give me a coo-ee and a wave.

The Germans finally decided to take a break. Either that, or they were running low on ammunition. The order was given to move out and continue on to Mouquet Farm.

Joe and Rob caught up with Keith but Johnno was nowhere to be seen. Some days later he was discovered in a gutter beside the road. There wasn't much left of him; it was obvious a shell had exploded very close to the poor bastard; it was only his dog tag that made the identification possible. Now there were three.

They dug in with the farm buildings in their sight four hundred yards in front of their line. The days ahead would be horrendous.

Charles Bean wrote:

> *The reader must take for granted many of the conditions – the flayed land, shell–hole bordering shell–hole, corpses of young men lying against the trench walls or in shell–holes; some – except for the dust settling on them – seeming to sleep; others torn in half; others rotting, swollen and discoloured.*
>
> *Charles Bean*, The Australian Imperial Force in France, 1916, Official History of Australia in the War of 1914–1918, Volume III, p. 728

The Farmer's Slaughter

Chapter 16

The Australian 4th Division including the 15th Battalion was finding things very tough; the German artillery was constantly shelling with uncanny accuracy. It became impossible to catch any sleep as the ground was wet and muddy. The boys renamed the farm "Mucky Farm". Others down the line called it "Moo Cow Farm" no matter what it was called, it was a living hell.

The Australians lost 23,000 men during the battle of Pozieres. Not many towns back home boasted a population of 23,000 plus. These catastrophic losses made it more difficult for the Anzacs to continue, but continue they did.

Initially, the 1st, 2nd, and 4th Divisions didn't receive reinforcements in any great numbers, but diggers who had been convalescing in the hospital were released to join their comrades at Moo Cow Farm. One of those released was Jimmie Pearson. Jimmie had been wounded at Fromelles when a piece of shrapnel had pierced his right thigh. The wound wasn't critical but nevertheless, he remained in the hospital for a few weeks. The wound had healed well enough for him to join the 15th Battalion at Mouquet Farm.

He reported to the Battalion Commander, the newly appointed Lieutenant Colonel James Jones.

'Private Pearson reporting for duty, sir.'

'Where did you come from, soldier?'

'The 30th, sir.'

'Were you at Fromelles?'

'Yes sir, that's where I got wounded.'

'Right, well you can join the 4th platoon. There's a couple of Abos there, so you'll fit right in.'

'Yes sir, and how do I find the black fellas?'

'Are you being insolent, soldier?'

'No, sir, not at all. That's what we call each other.'

'Is it? All right I'll arrange my sergeant to take you over. You're just in time for a fresh assault on the farm. The bloody Germans are proving very difficult to remove.'

Yes sir, thank you, sir.'

Sergeant Mills guided Jimmie to the spot in the trench where Joe, Keith, and Rob were resting up before the push.

'I have a reinforcement for you, Corporal; his name is Jimmie Pearson. I'll leave you to introduce him to the others in your platoon.'

'Just the one? I thought they were going to get us more than one,' complained Rob.

'You probably still will get more, but that's it for the moment.'

Rob looked at his new man.

'Well son, if you can fight anywhere near as good as my mate Joe here, you're most welcome.'

'All us Abos are great fighters, Corporal. We're all the same.'

'Fuck off private, don't get smart with me or I'll put you on body disposal full time.'

'Sorry sir, it's just that I get a little frustrated the way I'm treated sometimes.'

'Everybody is treated as an equal in this mob, and you're no different. I don't care what fucking colour your skin is.'

'Where are you from?' asked Joe.

'Sydney.'

'Ah, another Redfern boy.'

'Don't you start!'

'What do you mean?'

'It seems every bloody Aboriginal in New South Wales comes from bloody Redfern or so most people think.'

'Sorry mate, but a lot of us do live there.'

'Yeah, I suppose you're right. What about you? Where's your mob from?'

'Tassie, the Huon Valley.'

'Haven't heard of the Huon Valley. Where is it?'

'South, way down south.'

106

'Must be fucking cold.'

'Yeah, it gets a little cool in winter.'

'Do you get snow?'

'Yeah, not all the time, but we get our fair share.'

'What was the whopper you told the enlistment officer to get involved in this little picnic?' asked Joe.

'I told him I was half Scottish.'

'And he believed you? I'm surprised you're not wearing a fucking kilt to keep the charade up.' Joe laughed.

'How about you mate, what was the big fib you told?'

'I said my grandfather was an English sealer.'

'Do you ever wonder why we bothered? I mean, here we are in this stinking mud with fucking rats gnawing at our toes and the Krauts blasting us, trying their hardest to blow us to buggery.'

'Yeah, I often wonder why in the fuck did I try so hard to join the bloody army. You and I could have been living at home earning a reasonable living and being as safe as houses.'

'Well it's too late now, and at least we're making six bob a day.'

Rob approached the two Aboriginal warriors with new orders.

'Right boys, our platoon has been given the task of scouting no man's land to ascertain if there's a better than even chance for the battalion to make another push on the farmhouse. We go over the top in fifteen minutes so make sure your rifle is clean, and the bayonet is fixed. Take half a dozen grenades with you. Understand?'

'Yes mate,' they both replied.

The time came, and Rob signalled to the fifteen men under his charge to slowly climb the parapet and slide across the muddy bog on their bellies. A crescent moon made their advance stealth-like. The stench of rotting corpses from both sides was overpowering, and the ubiquitous rats were devouring the flesh of their fallen comrades as the platoon slithered past the ghoulish scene heading for the enemy's lines.

'Right, we've got another two hundred yards to the Krauts' trench. Once we get within eyesight, we need to record where the machine guns are located and how far back the big guns are positioned.'

Just then they heard several loud explosions.

'Shit, they must have seen us,' whispered Jimmie.

The Germans weren't firing mortars; they were firing flares. The dark night became illuminated, and the platoon's position was being compromised.

'Just keep your heads down and don't fucking move. With any luck they won't see us. When the light from the flare dims, head for a shell crater,' ordered Rob.

The platoon gradually moved into shell craters. They had no trouble finding a vacant hole; there were almost as many craters as dead bodies. The biggest problem they encountered was the amount of water in each crater. They had to stand in a muddy stinking quagmire ensuring their 303s and ammo kept dry.

'Fucking hell, this water smells putrid,' complained Joe.

'Everything around this fucking farm smells putrid,' said Jimmie.

'I can feel something against my bloody leg. Oh shit, it's a fucking corpse. Let's get out of here and find a better hole,' Joe said.

The two indigenous soldiers clambered out of the crater and began heading for an alternative position ten yards away. They were close to the lip when the Germans fired another volley of flares. Despite their natural night camouflage a Kraut machine gunner spotted them and let fire. Jimmie rolled into the crater unscathed; however, Joe got hit in his left arm and thigh. Jimmie pulled him in and made a couple of tourniquets to stem the flow of blood.

'You'll be all right mate, we'll stay here for a little while to let you settle down, then we'll head back for our line. We need to get you to the dressing station so they can assess your wounds. Knowing you, you'll be up and about in no time.'

'Thanks Jimmie. I must admit I feel pretty crook.'

Jimmie pulled his mate out of the crater and dragged him back the two hundred yards to the battalion's line. He was immediately taken to the dressing station where he was assessed and then moved back to the field hospital in Ypres. Joe was repatriated to England where he was treated at the 1st Australian Auxiliary Hospital at Harefield. The initial prognosis was that he would lose his arm and possibly his leg. Over the following weeks with magnificent care from the medical staff, they were able to repair both wounds without the need for amputation.

Joe was then moved to an Australian hospital in Dartford to convalesce for a further seven months. By the end of May 1917 he had full mobility and was shipped back to France.

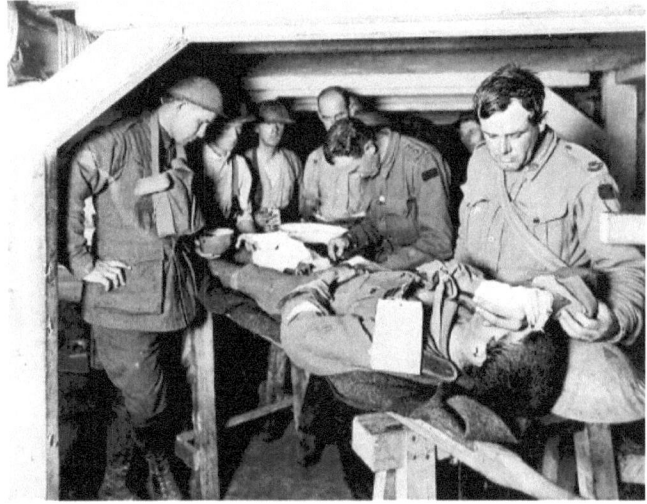

Clearing Station

Rob, Keith and Jimmie continued on the fight to capture the farm, but despite their best efforts, along with the 4th Division they were finally relieved, exhausted and battle weary. The 1st Division replaced them and although some gains were made, it was at a cost of heavy losses. The 1st Division was virtually destroyed and was relieved by the 2nd Division who after four days of intensive fighting withdrew, having lost many men. The 4th Division returned and again Rob, Keith and Jimmie were in the firing line. General Gough used the ANZACs seven times to try to capture Moo Cow Farm at a cost of 23,000 casualties. These atrocious figures were incurred between July 23rd and September 3rd, 1916.

Like a Bull in a China Shop
Bullecourt

Chapter 17

The First Battle of Bullecourt lasted all of one day and was an unmitigated disaster. The date was April 11, 1917. The 4th Division suffered badly, necessitating the force to withdraw from the battle for a period of some months. Who was responsible for the disaster? General Hubert Gough. Australian Command was furious with Gough's tactics, including the use of recently developed and untested tanks against the strongest defensive line on the entire Western Front; the Hindenburg Line.

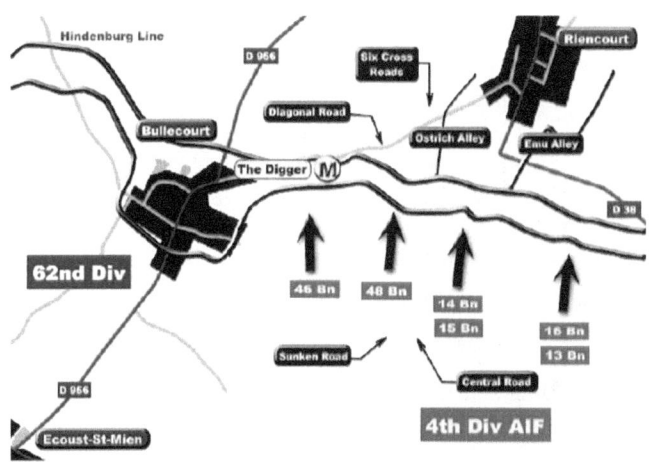

Gough, the commander of the Fifth Army, allowed himself to be convinced by his subordinates that Mark II and I tanks could be used to clear a path for his attacking infantry. This meant he could refrain from launching the usual heavy artillery bombardment prior to the attack. The tanks used lacked heavy armour plating and were designed as a training vehicle yet, they were expected to proceed across no man's land and flatten the immense lines of barbed wire laid out in front of the enemy trenches.

Despite the misgivings of Australian commanders, Gough insisted on his plan of attack go ahead. Even with evidence of the unreliability of the tanks, which failed to get within one mile of the jumping-off point by the time the attack was first scheduled, Gough immediately decided to reschedule the attack for the following morning using the tanks as originally planned.

The Australians weren't surprised that only four of the eleven tanks were in position at the scheduled start time. The tanks were so slow over the muddy terrain they were passed by the foot soldiers who reached the German defences well before the British Tanks that were meant to support them.

The 4th and 12th Brigades of the 4th Australian Division, despite the failure of the tanks, showed remarkable courage and ability and achieved what most observers believed was impossible, by breaking into a section the enemy trenches.

Their occupation was short-lived, for the Germans showered them with shells and blasted them with their deadly Mauser machine guns. The Australian artillery was remiss in not supporting them, resulting in enormous losses of the Anzacs who were the first troops ever to break the Hindenburg Line.

The animosity between the Australian and British Command was intensified after the First Battle of Bullecourt. The casualty figures could have and should have, been a lot lower.

The 12th Brigade went in 2,000 strong and suffered 950 casualties.

The 4th Brigade attacked with 3,000 and sustained 2,339 casualties!

Even by the standards of the Western Front at this time, a loss rate of 66 per cent was shocking. No wonder the 4th Division was withdrawn and took no further part in the action for months. Included in the casualties were some 1,250 men who were captured; approximately a third of all Australians were captured during the war.

'Bullecourt, more than any other battle, shook the confidence of Australian soldiers in the capacity of the British command: the errors, especially on April 10th and 11th, were obvious to almost everyone.'

Charles Bean. Official Historian

Second Battle of Bullecourt

The Guns at Bullecourt

This battle was more conventional but even more ferocious. It began on May 3rd and lasted for more than a fortnight.

Bullecourt was not an entirely British fiasco; Australian command was equally guilty of poor leadership and very questionable tactics. The Australian artillery failed the attacking infantry in both battles. Ironically Charles Bean forecast this would happen.

During the first Battle of Bullecourt artillery headquarters refused requests to support the attacking troops. Their excuse; they did not know where the Anzacs were exactly located.

This enabled the German machine gunners to rip into the advancing Australian troops, causing diabolical casualties.

Finally, the Australian artillery opened up, but their shells landed directly on the Australian positions. Many diggers died from so-called friendly fire.

The Army Intelligence did not uncover the fact that the German defence had massive machine gun batteries in front of and on each flank of the attacking British and Australian troops.

Accurate artillery bombardments would have lessened the firepower of the Germans.

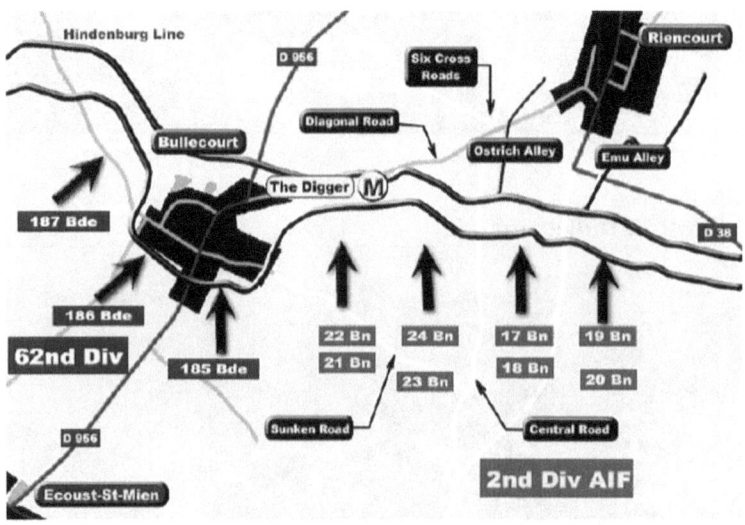

One of the fundamental lessons in war is to learn from one's mistakes. Incredibly, in planning for the Second Bullecourt, the attack plan completely ignored one of the major factors in the failure of the first operation: the flanking machine-gun fire brought down from the neighbouring village of Quéant.

As a result, these guns heavily attacked the Australian 5th Brigade when they came into view of the Quéant defenders. The casualty rate was so high that the 5th Brigade was ordered to withdraw. They never made it to the Hindenburg Line.

When the decision was made by the Australian Command to cancel the attack on April 10th, as the promised tanks had not arrived, the cancellation was not passed onto the British 62nd Division. Consequently, British troops were sent into Bullecourt village and were annihilated by the German machine gun defence. The British lost 162 men needlessly.

Both the Australians and the British fought side by side in ferocious battles and demonstrated their courage and tenacity against fierce defenders. Finally, the Germans withdrew.

Two officers who survived the onslaught at Bullecourt were Generals Gough and Haig.

Gough was the dashing ex-cavalryman, demanding that his subordinates demonstrate the "offensive spirit" always with an eye on the far horizon and the "big push". He was desperate to capture Bullecourt to ensure that Haig's offer of command of the Flanders campaign was confirmed.

Haig was also ex-cavalry. He was determined that the Flanders plan would proceed. Haig urged Gough to continue his attacks on Bullecourt to demonstrate to the French that British forces were continuing to apply pressure to the Germans and thereby retain French support for his objectives.

Pity the poor soldiers who, as a result, became casualties.

The Boys Are Back in Town

Chapter 18

After the fury and intensity of Mouquet Farm, the 4th Division was granted relief from the Western Front. They would no longer hear the sound of relentless artillery or suffer the constant stench of rotting bodies; light duties enabled them to recover.

Their numbers were much depleted; those who had survived the carnage were tired, sore and bruised both physically and mentally.

Major General Holmes, Commander of the Division, decided that two weeks leave would be granted. When British troops were given leave they were able to return home to their family and sweethearts. This luxury was not available to the Australians and New Zealanders; home was halfway around the world. The best alternative was making regular visits to Poperinge and partaking in the various activities available to war-weary soldiers.

Rob, Keith and Jimmie decided they would visit Pops, having spent two days in Ypres. The ancient town had been largely destroyed with not much available for soldiers on leave, and besides, they were just as likely to be hit by a German shell in Ypres as they were on the front.

They arrived in the late afternoon having caught a ride with a supply truck. Pops hadn't changed since their last visit. The town was awash with motor vehicles carrying supplies and troops either arriving from or leaving for the Front. Soldiers from the four corners of the Earth were swaggering along the cobblestones looking to get up to some serious mischief.

'Well, boys what do you want to do? We can check into our salubrious digs, clean up and hit the town or we could lie down on our stretchers and catch up with the latest edition of *Wipers Times* or *The War Illustrated*,' suggested Rob.

No. 3. Vol. I.   Monday, 6th March, 1916.   Price 200 Francs.

Editorial.

Firstly, we must apologise to our name and subscribers for the delay in bringing out our third number. Owing to the inclemency of the weather our rollers became completely demoralised, also the jealousy of our local competitors, Messrs. Hun and Co, reached an acute stage, and brought some of the wall down on our machine. But we have surmounted all these difficulties by obtaining, on the hire-purchase system, a beautiful Cropper? (I think that's the name) machine. This machine is jewelled in every hole, and has only been obtained at fabulous expense. So that we are once more able to resume our efforts towards peace, and by still telling the truth to our subscribers we hope to retain their confidence, which may have been shaken by pernicious utterings of the Yellow Press during our silence. Our great insurance scheme met with instant success, and we have already paid out three sums of 11.7 owing to an unfortunate accident on the Zillebeke Bund, where a celebrated firm of commission agents took the knock. At the urgent request of the painting staff we have just inspected our new machine. It is certainly a ghastly looking arrangement, and we hesitate to trust our ewe lamb in it's rapacious maw, but as it is either that or no ewe lamb we'll risk it. We hear that the war (to which we alluded guardedly in our first number), is proceeding satisfactorily, and we hope shortly to be able to announce that it is a going concern. So for the time being there we will leave it, and turn to graver subjects. We regret that there is still reason to deplore the inability, inefficiency, ineptitude and inertia of our City Fathers with regard to the condition of the roads (these are mostly up still)

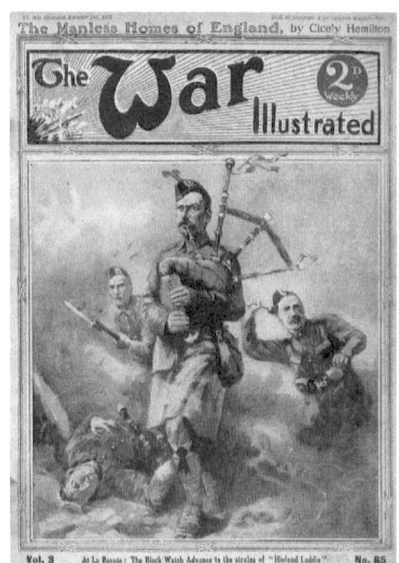

'To tell you the truth Rob, I'm leaning towards going into town and spending some time at Talbot House. After all, we've been through lately, I think we need some quiet time to relax,' said Jimmie.

'Yeah, I think I'm with you Jimmie,' said Keith.

'Okay, it's Talbot House for the first night and maybe some slap and tickle later on in the week,' said Rob.

The three diggers made their way to camp, showered, and put on recently laundered uniforms.

They walked into the town and headed for the Toc H, otherwise known as Tubby's place. Tubby was the resident chaplain and founder of Talbot House, and he was also a willing listener and a very wise counsel.

Tubby Clayton

The battle-weary soldiers entered Talbot House. A large vase of flowers had been placed on a majestic hall stand; the men stopped and smelt the sweet scent of the lilies. The only smells they had experienced in recent times were the stench from rotting corpses and the omnipresent odour of cordite from the constant shelling.

Tubby greeted them, inviting the Australians into the main sitting room. Vases of flowers were everywhere as were soldiers from Britain, Canada, New Zealand, and Australia. One of the principles of Talbot House was that rank was left at the front door. The soldiers' refuge was known as 'Everyman's Club'.

Tubby invited the boys to take a seat on the three-seater lounge. He chose to sit in an armchair. What a difference from the dirty, stinky, boggy trenches they had called home for the past few months! There were Persian rugs on the floor and beautiful curtains draped over the large bay windows

119

'Well, lads, I take it you've had a pretty tough time of it lately. Where have you been fighting?'

'Pozieres, Mouquet Farm and Bullecourt,' answered Keith.

'My God, you have been doing it tough. I know we lost many good men in those battles.'

'That we did, far too many. Our battalion has been badly damaged. Many of the cobbers we came over here with won't be going home, none will be more sorely missed than our good mates Johnno and Bill.' said Keith.

'Who were they?' asked Tubby.

'Johnno was just an ordinary good bloke who enlisted for the bloody war then he goes and gets himself killed.'

Bill was an Aboriginal like Jimmie here. He was a bloody good soldier and a great bloke.

'Well, we're still here I'm just lucky or unlucky depends how you look at it. I was accepted into this army despite my race.' said Jimmie.

'Why do you say that Jimmie?'

'The Australian Government banned our people from joining up; they figure you have to be a citizen to fight for your country.'

'Now I'm even more baffled. Why aren't you citizens?'

'I think they figure Aboriginals are bloody savages and wouldn't know how to vote. We're not allowed to drink alcohol and can't travel without permission as far as I know; I've never really tried.'

'So how did you enlist?'

'I lied about my race. As far as the army is concerned I'm a half-caste.'

'So you must be pretty upset about all this?'

'Yeah, I'm pretty pissed off the way the government treats us. We settled Australia well before the white man, and the buggers just come over and take our land. I'm hoping by fighting over here they might recognize our efforts. We're more bloody Australian than anyone.'

'Well, I'm shocked. I had no idea. I wish you well, Jimmie, and I hope they treat you like the hero you are when you return home.'

'Changing the subject, Tubby, we were hoping to borrow some books from the library while we're here, if that's okay?' Keith asked.

'Why, of course. Follow me and I'll show you where it is.'

The three diggers followed the pastor into the library.

'Do you have any preferences, gentlemen?'

'I'm rather fond of Rudyard Kipling,' said Rob.

'You're in luck. We have several Kipling books. I'd better check to see whether we have any on the shelves, as he's rather popular. Ah, we have *The Jungle Book* and a new release called *The Light That Failed*.'

'That'll do me, Tubby, thank you.'

'What about you, Jimmie? What do you like reading?'

'I don't know, Tubby. I can't say I've ever read a book. I usually read magazines and comics.'

'May I make a suggestion?'

'Sure.'

'*Private Spud Tamson*, by Captain R. W. Campbell. I've read it and it's a damn good read. It's very popular.'

'Thanks Tubby, I'll let you know how I go.'

'Well, that only leaves you, Keith; what's your preference?'

'H. G. Wells.'

'You've obviously read him before?'

'I read *War of the Worlds* some time back; I've been an admirer ever since.'

'The only H. G. Wells available presently is his latest release, *The World Set Free*. I haven't read it yet but I've heard good reports.'

'Thanks, Tubby.'

The three diggers retired to the sitting room, where a pot of tea and three ornate cups were waiting for them. The trio began reading.

They had entered Talbot House at 5pm and didn't leave until after midnight. All had progressed more than halfway through their respective books. Jimmie had discovered a whole new world far away from the mayhem of the battlefield. *Private Spud* might have been his first but would certainly not be his last book.

They walked back to camp, entered their tent and not surprisingly were asleep within five minutes.

The three diggers went back into town the following morning, looking forward to a Devonshire tea at Café L' Esperance. The owners of the café introduced the English favourite, having had numerous requests from the Tommies and diggers who frequented the establishment since the war began.

As they consumed their scones, strawberry jam and cream washed down by English breakfast tea, they felt quite contented.

Talbot House was the next port of call, where they resumed their reading for the remainder of the day. All three had finished their books by 5pm.

'Well cobbers, it's been a very relaxing day. I'm starting to forget the bloody war already,' said Rob.

'Yeah, I know what you mean, Rob; only one more thing to do to finish off a bloody good day,' replied Keith.

'What's that Keith?' asked Jimmie.

'A visit to our favourite house of ill repute.'

'I'm up for that,' said Jimmie enthusiastically.

'Fair enough, let's head off to La Lanterne Rouge,' said Rob.

They entered the infamous establishment to be greeted by Madame Charlene.

'Good evening Messieurs, how may I be of service?'

'Madame, we are looking for pleasure,' said Rob.

'So, you have come to the right place; pleasure is our business. How long would you care to visit for?'

The three men looked at each other.

'What do you reckon, fellas? An hour?' asked Rob.

'Yeah, why not, let's do an hour,' said Jimmie.

'You okay with that Keith?' asked Rob.

'Yeah, that's fine. May as well enjoy ourselves good and proper.'

'One hour would suit us, Madam,' said Rob.

'Have you been here before?'

'Yes, we have, Madam.'

'Excellent, well you know what to do. The first thing is you pay me five francs each then you go to the lounge and choose a lady.'

They paid Madame Charlene and entered the salubrious lounge where several ladies in various states of undress were sitting on lounges waiting for their next patrons. Once the choices were made each soldier followed the young lady into a bedroom.

An hour later the boys met in the foyer, all looking very pleased with themselves.

Dreaming

Chapter 19

Jimmie had discovered the world of books, a world unknown to him a few days before. He returned to the Toc H intent on finding another book similar to *Private Spud*. Upon entering the club he headed for the library with great expectations. Tubby was cataloguing some new arrivals. Ironically, *Great Expectations* by Charles Dickens was the book Tubby recommended. It was nothing like *Captain Spud* but Tubby knew he would enjoy it.

The pastor asked Jimmie if he would care to join him for a cup of tea in his office. This invitation was most unusual as Tubby regarded his own space as sacrosanct.

Once the tea had been prepared and poured Tubby broached the subject of Aboriginal culture.

'Jimmie, I was amazed and in fact concerned to hear how unfairly your country is treating you and your people.'

'Don't be too concerned Tubby. I'm sure things will change once this bloody war is over. Excuse my language.'

'Don't worry about your language, mate. I hear a lot worse here every bloody day.'

'The problem is the white man doesn't understand the Aboriginal culture, and to be honest we've not been very good at explaining it to him.'

'Well, why don't you try explaining it to me? I'm very keen to understand.'

'Okay, well everything begins with the 'Dreaming' or 'Tjukurrpa'. In your language, it means 'to see and understand the law'. Dreaming is the foundation of our spiritual lives, which can be traced to our Great Spirit ancestors.

'Dreaming stories passes on important knowledge, cultural values and our belief systems to our later generations.'

'How do you pass on this knowledge? We have books, but I understand you have no written language.'

'We have song, dance, painting and storytelling; we have used these methods since arriving in the great southern land.'

'And that was a very long time ago I believe.'

'It is our understanding that our people have occupied what you call Australia for over 50,000 years. This is what the white man has told us from their discoveries.'

'What discoveries Jimmie?'

'Digging in sites where we used to live and uncovering bones and artefacts.'

'Are you able to tell me any Dreamtime stories?'

'Not specifically, but I'll try to give you the essence. In most stories of the Dreaming, the Ancestor Spirits came to the Earth in human form and as they moved through the land, they created the animals, plants, rocks and other forms of the land that we know today. They also created the relationships between groups and individuals to the land.

'Once the ancestor spirits had created the world, they changed into trees, the stars, rocks, watering holes and other objects. These are the sacred places of our culture and have special properties. Because our ancestors did not disappear at the end of the Dreaming but remained in these sacred sites, the Dreaming is never-ending, linking the past and the present, the people and the land.'

'So Dreaming is your equivalent to the Christian Bible?'

'To some extent. I was raised a Catholic so I was exposed to the Bible during my school years I never read it cover to cover though. We believe the Earth was a flat surface, in darkness; a dead, silent world. Unknown forms of life were asleep, below the surface of the land. Then the supernatural Ancestor Beings broke through the crust of the earth from below, with tumultuous force.

'The sun rose out of the ground. The land received light for the first time.

'The supernatural beings resembled creatures or plants and were half human. They moved across the barren surface of the world. They travelled hunted and fought and changed the form of the land. In their journeys, they created the landscape, the mountains, the rivers, the trees, waterholes, plains and sand hills. They made us, the people; we are descendants of the Dreamtime ancestors. They made the ant, grasshopper, emu, eagle, crow, parrot, wallaby, kangaroo, lizard, snake, and all food plants. They made the natural elements: water, air, and fire. They made all the celestial bodies: the sun, the moon and the stars. Then, wearied from all their activity, the mythical creatures sank back into the earth and returned to their state of sleep.

'Sometimes their spirits turned into rocks or trees or a part of the landscape. I suppose it is similar to your own Dreaming, Tubby.'

'What do you mean?'

'Your Dreaming is in the Bible, Genesis to be exact. You must have a Bible handy so let's compare.'

Tubby reached for his Bible and opened the holy text at Genesis.

The Beginning

In the beginning God created the heavens and the earth.

Now, the earth was formless and empty, darkness was over the surface of the deep, and the Spirit of God was hovering over the waters.

And God said, "Let there be light," and there was light.

God saw that the light was good, and he separated the light from the darkness.

God called the light "day," and the darkness he called "night." And there was evening, and there was morning—the first day.

And God said, "Let there be a vault between the waters to separate water from water."

So God made the vault and separated the water under the vault from the water above it. And it was so.

God called the vault "sky." And there was evening, and there was morning—the second day.

And God said, "Let the water under the sky be gathered to one place, and let dry ground appear." And it was so.

God called the dry ground "land," and the gathered waters he called "seas." And God saw that it was good.

Then God said, "Let the land produce vegetation: seed-bearing plants and trees on the land that bear fruit with seed in it, according to their various kinds." And it was so.

The land produced vegetation: plants bearing seed according to their kinds and trees bearing fruit with seed in it according to their kinds. And God saw that it was good.

And there was evening, and there was morning—the third day.

And God said, "Let there be lights in the vault of the sky to separate the day from the night, and let them serve as signs to mark sacred times, and days and years, and let them be lights in the vault of the sky to give light on the earth." And it was so.

God made two great lights—the greater light to govern the day and the lesser light to govern the night. He also made the stars.

God set them in the vault of the sky to give light on the earth, to govern the day and the night, and to separate light from darkness. And God saw that it was good.

And there was evening, and there was morning—the fourth day.

And God said, "Let the water teem with living creatures, and let birds fly above the earth across the vault of the sky."

So God created the great creatures of the sea and every living thing with which the water teems and that moves about in it, according to their kinds, and every winged bird according to its kind. And God saw that it was good.

God blessed them and said, "Be fruitful and increase in number and fill the water in the seas, and let the birds increase on the earth."

And there was evening, and there was morning—the fifth day.

And God said, "Let the land produce living creatures according to their kinds: the livestock, the creatures that move along the ground, and the wild animals, each according to its kind." And it was so.

God made the wild animals according to their kinds, the livestock according to their kinds, and all the creatures that move along the ground according to their kinds. And God saw that it was good.

Then God said, "Let us make mankind in our image, in our likeness, so that they may rule over the fish in the sea and the birds in the sky, over the livestock and all the wild animals and over all the creatures that move along the ground."

God created mankind in his own image, in the image of God he created them; male and female he created them

God blessed them and said to them, "Be fruitful and increase in number; fill the earth and subdue it. Rule over the fish in the sea and the birds in the sky and over every living creature that moves on the ground."

Then God said, "I give you every seed-bearing plant on the face of the whole earth and every tree that has fruit with seed in it. They will be yours for food.

And to all the beasts of the earth and all the birds in the sky and all the creatures that move along the ground—everything that has the breath of life in it—I give every green plant for food." And it was so.

God saw all that he had made, and it was very good. And there was
evening, and there was morning—the sixth day.

'Yes, I see the similarity. Rob you also told me Aboriginals are precluded from owning land.'

'We don't own the land. The land owns us. The land is my mother. My mother is the land. The land is the starting point to where it all began. It is like picking up a piece of dirt, and saying this is where I started and this is where I will go. The land is our food, our culture, our spirit, and identity. We don't have boundaries like fences, as farmers do. We have spiritual connections.'

'Jimmie, it's been an enlightening conversation, mate. I've learnt a lot, and I thank you for being so open with me.'

'I enjoyed the time with you Tubby. I better go and find Rob and Keith. It's our last night in Poperinge.'

'You all be careful. And don't forget your book, Jimmie, I know you will enjoy reading Mr Dickens bring it back during your next visit.'

The Third Battle of Ypres

Chapter 20

The three diggers met back at Poperinge camp to begin planning their last night.

'Is there any disagreement on what we do tonight boys?' asked Rob.

'None whatsoever. It could be our last chance to be with a woman for a very long time,' said Keith.

'No argument from me,' said Jimmie.

'Right then, I suggest we have dinner at A la Poupée and then visit Madam Charlene at La Lanterne Rouge.'

'Sounds like a bonza last night to me.'

'Me too,' said Jimmie.

The next morning the three soldiers were brought back to reality with the sound of reveille.

The battalion then began their journey to Ypres where they would muster before the next great battle – The Third Battle of Ypres.

London buses, shipped to France, being used to move up a division of Australian troops.

The convoy of London buses arrived in the afternoon, having survived the roads and the constant shelling. Unfortunately, two buses didn't survive; German aircraft demolished them killing all on board. Rob, Keith and Jimmie were on the bus immediately behind one of the buses that got hit.

Once in Ypres, Rob and his mates were sitting around a campfire boiling a billy of tea when they heard a familiar voice.

'Who do you have to kill around here to get a fucking cup of tea?'

'Joe, you're back. How the fuck are you, cobber?'

'I'm good now. Not so good a while back as you all know.'

'Sit down and I'll make you a nice cup of tea,' said Jimmie.

'So mate, we didn't think you would make it back. We were sure they put you on a ship back home short of a leg or two,' said Keith.

'Bloody hell, I was pretty fucking close to losing my leg; I could have lost an arm too. The Aussie doctors at Harefield were fantastic; they weren't going to give in. They persevered and lo and behold I'm all in one piece ready to be blown up again.'

'Let's bloody hope not. Here, drink your tea. It's good for you,' said Jimmie.

'Oh, shit did you feel that? It's starting to rain. That's all we bloody need. More rain and more fucking mud.'

The 4th Division was stationed in Ypres, waiting to be deployed. The Australian troops could hear the Pilckem Ridge Battle raging in the distance. They were thankful it wasn't them fighting in the wet and muddy conditions. Their time would come at Menin Road.

Menin Road

Passchendaele

The next day would be the beginning of the 'Battle of Mud' as the Third Battle of Ypres became known. It was also known as The Battle of Passchendaele.

Few battles encapsulate World War One better than the Battle of Passchendaele.

Sir Douglas Haig was the Chief of Staff and British Commander.

He devised a plan whereby an attempt would be made to break through Flanders. Haig had planned a similar attack in 1916, but the Battle of the Somme had him preoccupied at the time. It was one year later before Haig could launch his attack. The main aim was to break through to the coast of Belgium so that German submarine pens could be destroyed. Admiral Jellicoe, Admiral of the British Fleet, had already advised both Haig and the British Government that the loss of shipping; primarily merchant, could not be sustained and that Britain would face severe problems in 1918 if such losses continued. Haig's plan, to sweep through Flanders to the coast, did not initially receive support from Britain's Prime Minister, David Lloyd George, but as the Allies had no other credible plan, he reluctantly gave his permission for Haig to carry out his intention. The two men detested each other.

Haig also had another reason for proceeding with his plan. He was under the delusion that the morale of the German army was very low after having been soundly defeated at Messines. It was his belief that the Allies would march through Flanders without much resistance.

On July 18th 1917 came a heavy artillery barrage as 3000 artillery guns firing 4,000,000 shells were launched, devised to destroy German lines. The Germans were entrenched in deep bunkers constructed to withstand such an attack. When the ten-day barrage ceased, they knew a British attack was imminent and prepared for the battle.

The infantry attack started on July 31st. General Sir Hubert Gough's Fifth Army led the main assault. To their left were units from the French First Army led by General François Paul Anthoine, and to Gough's right was the Second Army led by the victor of Messines, General Sir Herbert Plumer.

Passchendaele Mud

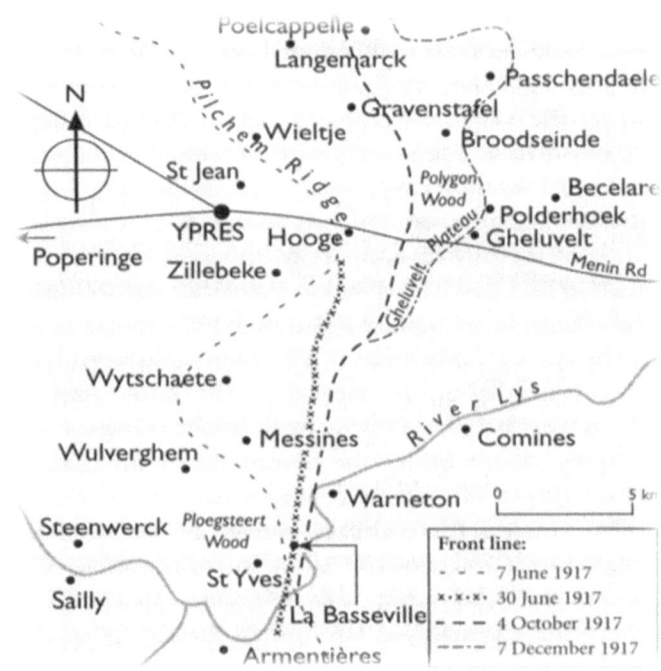

The Germans were fully prepared for the Allied attack, launched across an eleven-mile front, and the British made only small gains. Then, in the early days of August, the area was saturated with the heaviest rain the region had seen in thirty years. Flanders became effectively a swamp; tanks sent forward to help the infantry got stuck in the mud, and some actually sank. Infantry soldiers found movement very difficult. The impact of the artillery bombardment had destroyed the drainage systems of the region, which greatly added to the problem. The shell craters made by the Allied shelling filled with water, and did not allow advancing men the opportunity to take refuge. The fields became impassable. This truly was no man's land.

Haig blamed the lack of progress, not on the abnormal weather and the shocking conditions, but on General Gough. Haig moved Gough and his men to a position further north and promoted General Plumer to take charge of the battle. Plumer's tactics were different to Gough's. He aimed to achieve small gains that could be permanently held as opposed to Gough's apparent desire for one major sweeping movement designed to bring victory. Plumer fought a series of small battles within Flanders – the Battle of Menin Road, the Battle of Polygon Wood and the Battle of Broodseinde— all fought by valiant Australian troops. These battles were fought between September and October 1917. The Australians' success gave British forces the advantage in the tactically significant territory to the east of Ypres.

Haig was buoyed by these victories and believed that German morale was on the decline. His confidence boosted, he ordered the attack on Passchendaele Ridge.

Between October 9th and October 12th, two battles were fought; Poelcappelle and the First Battle of Passchendaele. At this point in time the German soldiers who had been fighting on the Eastern Front had been moved to the Western Front; predominately Passchendaele Ridge.

Haig and Plumer's optimism soon waned, as the Germans, with the aid of mustard gas and sheer numbers, repelled the Allied attack.

Passchendaele

Haig would not concede that the attack had been a complete failure. In late October three further Allied attacks were made on Passchendaele Ridge by the British, Australian and New Zealanders. The Canadians were brought in to relieve the exhausted troops and on November 6th, 1917, they took Passchendaele village.

Passchendaele had been a very costly battle for very little gain. The Allies lost 310,000 men and the Germans 260,000. Haig was heavily criticised for the attack. He had failed to modify his plans or to consider the atrocious weather. He also dismissed the fact that the Eastern Front troops had joined the affray.

Haig argued that the Allies could and did suffer greater casualties than the Germans, but this was acceptable on the basis that the Americans had joined the war and would more than replace their losses.

The loved ones back home that received the dreaded telegrams might have disagreed with him.

'It was simply the mud which defeated us on Tuesday. The men did splendidly to get through it as they did. But the Flanders mud, as you know, is not a new invention. It has a name in history - it has defeated other armies before this one...' (quoted in Bean, Official History, Vol IV, p 908.)

Menin Road

Chapter 21

The day began like every other day at Ypres. The bugle sounded reveille the four Australian diggers, along with the rest of the 4th Division, woke to the sound of pounding rain and boots of the early risers squelching through the thick slimy mud on their way to the mess tent.

'Fucking hell, I hope they send us out to take on the Krauts pretty soon,' complained Jimmie.

'Why mate, are you keen to get your balls blown off by some Jerry machine gun?' asked Keith.

'Well no, but I'm so fucking bored. All we do all day is sit around doing fuck all. I don't even have a book to read.'

'You've become quite the bookworm since you arrived here, haven't you?'

'Yeah, well it certainly relieves the boredom.'

Captain Bannister, their commander, had heard some of the conversations as he approached the group with some news.

'Well, lads I've got a plan that will relieve you of all the boredom you've all been moaning about.'

'Good morning, sir, what plan would that be?' asked Rob.

'We've just received orders from High Command. We're being sent to take on the Germans down the road a bit.'

'Sorry sir, could you be a bit more explicit?' asked Rob.

'We're moving down to Menin Road to stop the Germans moving into Ypres.'

'I see, so when do we move?' asked Joe.

'In a couple of hours, so you better get cracking.'

The camp became a hive of activity with soldiers hitching up horses to gun carriages and ammunition wagons. Soldiers assembled on the Ypres end of Menin road ready for the march five miles down the track to where the Germans were waiting for them.

ANZACS Marching Along the Menin Road

As the Australians began their march along the Menin Road, they could hear the British bombardment of the German positions. General Plumer had ordered 3.5 million shells be fired to soften their resistance when the battle began in earnest.

'Bloody hell, by the sounds of it they'll be no fucking Germans left to fight,' said Rob.

'I don't know about that, there was plenty left at Pozieres and Moo Cow Farm after the artillery slammed them,' responded Keith.

'Yeah, the bastards seem to know how to dodge them.'

When the Australians arrived at Menin Ridge the ground was dry and all they could see was pockmarked earth and the remains of buildings and stone walls, resembling gravestones. The troops settled into their positions, knowing that when dawn broke they would be fighting for their lives. As soon as darkness fell so too did the rain. It was heavy and relentless within an hour or two the dry clay became a slimy sticky bog.

The plan was for the Australians to advance in three stages to take the designated Red, Blue and Green Lines drawn on a map by High Command. They anticipated the counter-attacks would come once they reached the Green Line.

'Fuck this, I can hardly lift my bloody boots they're so caked in mud,' complained Joe.

'Yeah, and I'm soaked to the skin. Not the best fighting conditions I must say,' said Rob.

To make matters worse the Germans began a savage barrage. Diggers were being blown to pieces, literally. Body parts were strewn all over the muddy battlefield. Most of their commanders were killed in the onslaught.

The British artillery opened up in retaliation; the smoke from the shells became so thick that it was almost impossible for the troops to find their way.

British Guns

The Allied troops did navigate their way only to find limited German resistance; they had been badly shaken by the British barrage. There were several skirmishes centred on the German pillboxes but overall it was a relatively easy victory. Many Germans surrendered, waving white handkerchiefs or bandages.

The four diggers were together in a crater created with the compliments of the British big guns. If they hadn't found refuge they would have joined their comrades and officers strewn about the mud.

'Well, what do we do now? If we leave our hole we'll be in the sights of the German machine guns; if we stay we'll be court-martialled for cowardice,' said Keith.

'We have to go forward. There's no other way,' recommended Jimmie.

The four cobbers made their way out and started to slither across the quagmire, their objective, the Green Line. To reach their goal they had to take out a German pillbox, which was wreaking havoc with relentless machine gunfire.

'Listen, fellas, I reckon Joe and I can get close enough to blow these bastards up. Rob, you and Keith cover us with rifle fire. What do you reckon? It's got to be worth a shot?' said Jimmie.

'Okay, if you're happy to give it a go,' said Rob.

'I wouldn't say we're fucking happy about it but it's the only chance we have of advancing to the Green Line.'

'Give us all your grenades I think we're going to need them.'

The two Aboriginal mates, loaded up with grenades and their trusty 303s, began their dangerous journey. They slid on their bellies, halting every ten yards or so to assess their position.

German Pillbox

After about half an hour they determined that they were close enough to execute their plan. Jimmie took the left-hand side of the pillbox, Joe, the right. Once in position, they gave each other a predetermined signal, a wave. Both soldiers pulled the pins from the grenades, waited five seconds and lobbed them in through the gun slit. Seconds later the grenades exploded. Quickly two more grenades were thrown and two more explosions were heard. They listened but couldn't hear a sound. Reasonably confident all had been killed, they moved around to the entrance, rifles at the ready. They entered the smoke-filled den only to find six dead German soldiers.

Dead German Soldiers inside the Pillbox

Once they were absolutely sure all the occupants had been killed they signalled to their platoon using their rifles to fire two shots, a five-second delay, and another two. Rob, Keith and the remainder of the platoon; twenty men in all, proceeded cautiously to the destroyed German fortification.

When the Battle of Menin Road was officially regarded as over, Australia had suffered 5,013 casualties. The four brothers in arms survived to fight another day.

Jimmie and Joe were recommended to receive a Victoria Cross, the highest distinction for gallantry. The requirement is that at least three witnesses verify the heroism, and the commanding officer submits the recommendation. In this case, there was no commanding officer but the entire platoon witnessed the event.

The Secretary for Defence in London considered the recommendation; however, it was decided that the appropriate award should be the Military Medal.

Despite many acts of heroism during the war not one indigenous soldier received the Victoria Cross. Sixty-four were awarded to Caucasian soldiers.

Surrender

Chapter 22

Rob, who had been promoted to corporal, led a group of twenty men including Jimmie, Joe, and Keith.

They were charged with taking the village of Passchendaele along with 5 Australian Divisions, 41 British Divisions, 4 Canadian and 1 New Zealand Division.

His platoon discovered they were trapped, surrounded by German troops.

'Well, what in the fuck do we do now, sir?' asked Keith.

'Don't call me sir you idiot, not here anyway. The way I see it we can fight our way back with the very strong possibility we will all be killed or we can bite the bullet as it were and hold up the white flag.'

'I don't think we carry a white flag Rob. Would a relatively clean white hankie do?' suggested Jimmie.

'So I take it mate, you're for surrendering?'

'Well, I prefer it to the other option.'

'What about you, Joe?'

'Yep, I'm all for living and taking my chances in a POW camp. At least, we'll still all be together.'

'Pass me that hankie, Jimmie.'

Rob tied the hankie to the end of his bayonet and raised it so the Germans could see. He heard a German voice yell out in broken English to throw their weapons out in front of them.

This the twenty men did. They were then instructed to stand up with their hands in the air.

Several German soldiers approached them with rifles pointed at the Australian diggers.

They were ordered to form a line three abreast and began marching to Passchendaele. Once they arrived in the ruined village, they were searched for other weapons. When their captors were sure there were no weapons concealed they were ordered to sit on the muddy ground and await further instructions.

At night the rain began falling and the temperature plummeted. There was no shelter so the Australians were soaked. They hadn't eaten for some hours but were offered no food. This was how the Australian POWs spent their first night in captivity.

The next morning they were assembled and given a lecture in German that nobody in the group could understand. They figured they were being told not to attempt to escape, or they'd be shot.

The German Guards then manhandled the POWs into one long column three abreast, and the eight-hour march to Lille began. The prisoners were not permitted to talk and the Germans decided when they could take toilet breaks. They were all marching on empty stomachs.

Rob and the boys were amazed how many prisoners there were. It wasn't just their platoon who had been captured; there was at least one hundred other soldiers, all Australian.

Australian POWs Marching Through Lille

The prisoners were herded into an open compound within a fort with very little shelter and no amenities. This facility served as an interim prison before they were transported to various POW camps in Germany.

The Germans ... put us in a fort at Lille. They never gave us anything. We may have had a slice of bread a day, nothing else. We were building dugouts, huts, carrying and loading shells. We had one slice of bread in the morning and at lunchtime a pot of soup, which was almost like water.

Private Horace Ganson, 16th Battalion, AIF

After about a week the prisoners were assembled. The German commandant read out each soldier's name and which POW camp they were assigned to. The four diggers who had been through so much together were hoping they would be allocated to the same camp. It was not to be, Rob and Keith were assigned to Senne camp in Germany, and Joe and Jimmie were sent to Zossen, a camp for Indians and other black and coloured prisoners.

Senne POW Camp

Zossen with Mosque

Joe and Jimmie boarded the transport train if you could call being shoved into a cattle cart with hardly enough room to scratch one's self boarding. Other occupants seemed to be Indian with a few Africans thrown into the mix.

They endured these conditions for two days. Many POWs were dehydrated and others had a fever. The two Australian Aboriginals survived the journey relatively unscathed.

Once the train pulled into the Zossen station and the German guards unloaded their human cargo, the prisoners were marched three kilometres to the camp. The fresh air was a welcome relief from the putrid air of the wagon but many POWs were having difficulties keeping up on the march. Their legs had weakened during the trip. Things got better once they reached the camp. The prisoners were processed and allocated identity numbers, they were showered and their uniforms were laundered. To their surprise, there were Irish prisoners also housed at Zossen; the only white men at the camp. However, the Germans segregated the white and black prisoners.

At the Kaiser's Pleasure

Chapter 23

Jimmie and Joe were relieved they had been assigned to the same hut, and they chose bunks next to each other. They knew they must stick together if they were going to get through this ordeal. Being the only Australians, let alone the only Aboriginals in Zossen, meant they were on their own in what could be, potentially, a very hostile environment.

The two men fitted into the daily regime well, and they were assigned to a work detail tending the vegetable garden. They enjoyed working in the large allotment knowing that some of the produce would end up on their plates.

After a period of six weeks, they still hadn't had the luxury of a cigarette or a book to read.

'Hey Joe, have you heard anything mentioned about Red Cross parcels?'

'No, I can't say that I have mate.'

It's just that we were told if we were captured we should expect to have Red Cross parcels delivered. Apparently, it's standard practice.'

'Are you going to broach the subject with Boris or should I?'

'Well Boris doesn't look all that approachable and I'd hate to get on the wrong side of the bastard.'

'Yeah, maybe we should leave it for a while and see whether they turn up.'

Boris was a very large man weighing about 220 pounds; he measured six-foot two in height. His bushy moustache gave him an almost comical appearance, but his temperament was fierce. POWs knew not to get on the wrong side of Boris.

Another month passed, and the Red Cross parcels had still not arrived.

'I have the strong feeling the parcels have been seconded by the fucking guards, mate,' said Joe.

'Yep, I don't care about the food so much, but I could really go a smoke right now.'

'I'm with you, cobber.'

'Bloody Germans.'

'Well, I suppose we're in here for the duration so we better get used to it,' said Jimmie.

'Yeah mate, unless we can escape but I reckon that's got hairs on it. We're so far inside Germany it's not funny.'

'Well, there's one good thing about all this.'

'Yeah, and what would that be?'

'No mud, no bullets whizzing past and no fucking shells trying to kill us.'

'True.'

The following day a supply van was driven into the quadrangle and began distributing Red Cross parcels to all the prisoners. The POWs couldn't believe their luck.

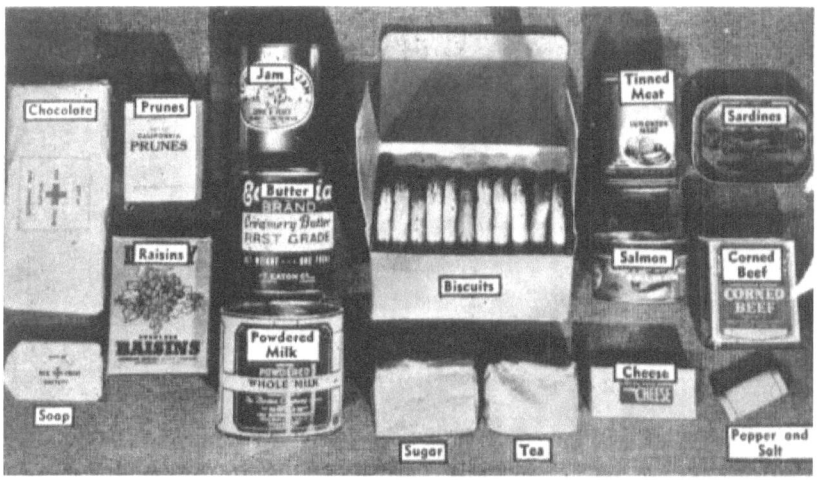

Contents Of Red Cross Comfort Parcel

The prisoners also received a ration of cigarettes, four packets each. Rationing would be essential, as they had no idea when the next parcel would arrive.

Also, distributed were woollen jumpers, scarves, and socks; the boys thought it was Christmas.

Just as Jimmie and Joe were sifting through the contents of their packages, Boris entered the hut and ordered the two Aboriginals to follow him to the commandant's office.

'Fuck, what have we done wrong?' whispered Joe.

'Fucked if I know.'

'No talking.'

They reached the office and were instructed to wait with Boris in the waiting room. There was a very pretty blonde girl typing. The boys hadn't seen a woman since Pops; they were quite taken aback by her beauty.

After a fifteen-minute wait, the secretary instructed the two Australians to enter the commandant's office. Boris was told to wait.

'Ah, our two black Australians. As you are aware there are many black prisoners here at Zossen but you two are the only black Australians. So what is it you are called?'

'Permission to speak, sir?' said Joe, having been instructed how he should address the commandant.

'Yes, permission granted, so what are you called?'

'We are called Aboriginals, sir.'

'Really, well that's very interesting. The reason I have called you here is to inform you that you will be transferred to Berlin tonight. It appears some of our scientists are interested in examining you both.'

'Yes, sir.'

'That will be all.'

The two diggers returned to their hut to gather what little they had.

At 9pm a large black Mercedes Benz arrived, and the two men were instructed to get into the back seat. Boris and another guard accompanied them.

The trip to Berlin was comfortable despite being forbidden to speak, a world away from the cattle wagons they had to endure on the trip to Zossen.

The trip took only an hour. The two Australians had no idea Zossen was so close to their enemy's capital.

The Mercedes pulled up outside a very impressive stone building called *The Museum of Anthropology*.

Boris and the other guard ordered the two prisoners out of the car and escorted them around the rear of the building. They all entered through a very nondescript door leading to a great hall filled with ancient Egyptian mummies and various stone carvings. The party then ascended a large staircase taking them to what seemed like offices lining a long corridor. The Australians were instructed to enter one of these rooms where they found two beds, a sink and a toilet. This was where Joe and Jimmie would be living for the next few weeks.

The door slammed shut behind them. A loud metal clang rang out, and the sound of the bolt sliding and the key turning in the lock dismissed any thoughts they were in for an easy time.

The two men lay down on their beds still dressed in their uniforms, looking at the ceiling and the solitary globe illuminating the room.

'What do you reckon they will do with us, mate?

'Dunno. I'm hoping they won't cut us open and see whether we're the same as a white man inside.'

'Jesus, don't say that. I'll start to worry.'

'Well, the commandant said scientists wanted to examine us. Why would they want to examine us for fuck sake?'

'Buggered if I know. I suppose we'll find out in the morning.'

'I think we should try to get some sleep. It could be a long day ahead of us.'

'Yeah, I think you're right. I'll turn the light off. Goodnight, mate.'

'Good night.'

'Shit, there's no light switch; it must be on the outside. I hope they don't leave it on all night.'

'So do I. Having a bloody light burning all night won't help us get a good night's sleep.'

The two prisoners closed their eyes and despite the light burning bright, fell asleep.

Next morning they were woken by the noise of the steel door being unlocked. A guard they hadn't seen before had two plates of porridge and some fresh fruit for their breakfast. Joe and Jimmie ate their breakfast, particularly enjoying the fruit. The guard, Helmut, returned with two tin cups of tea.

They felt thoroughly spoiled.

'I hope this isn't the last meal before execution,' said Joe.

'Don't even joke about it, mate.'

'I wasn't.'

Helmut returned and ordered the two men to wash and clean their teeth with the toiletries supplied. Once clean and presentable the men were escorted out of the cell and down the corridor. At the end of the passageway was a large laboratory. The men looked at each other with fear in their eyes. A distinguished-looking man, tall, with a closely cropped white beard, greeted them in a friendly manner. He had a white lab coat unbuttoned over what looked like an expensive tweed three-piece suit.

'Good morning gentlemen, welcome to my humble laboratory. My name is Doctor Ekstein; I am looking forward to examining you and discovering something more about the Australian Aboriginal. You may wait outside in the corridor, guard. I am sure everything will be fine. I will call you if I need you.'

'I don't think that's such a good idea, Doctor, I think I should remain here with you and the prisoners.'

'I insist.'

'Yes, Doctor.'

'Now, what are your names?'

'I'm Joe and this is Jimmie.'

'Well, men, follow me into my office.'

'Doctor, may we ask whether you intend to conduct any surgery on us?'

'Of course not! I just want to discover more about your race by questioning you. I would like to take some vital measurements but that would be the limit of my medical assessment.'

'Thank you, Doctor, we were both a bit worried.'

'Well, there's no need to worry, Jimmie.'

Doctor Ekstein examined both men, noting their height and other body measurements. He also measured their heads to try to determine the size of their brains.

'You are both in excellent health; you should live to a ripe old age.'

'Wonderful; that's as long as we don't get killed in action.'

'You're prisoners of war. I don't think there's much chance of that happening.'

Over the following two weeks, Dr Ekstein and the two Australians met daily. They discussed Aboriginal Dreamtime and life in Australia.

Both men had totally different lifestyles; Joe had worked on an apple orchard in the beautiful Huon Valley in Tasmania while Jimmie had lived in what was regarded as an Aboriginal ghetto in Redfern in Sydney, where he was a builder's labourer. Dr Ekstein was fascinated to hear about the lives they lived; it was so foreign to the life of most Germans.

The two prisoners were given more freedom at the museum than they would have endured at Zossen. They were both fascinated with the Egyptian exhibition as both had been to Egypt prior to being deployed to the Western Front.

Finally, the time came when they were due to return to Zossen and the camp regime. The last morning was spent in the lab with Doctor Ekstein. He recapped what he had learnt over the past fortnight and unusually read the men his conclusion to the report he had written.

In essence, he concluded that both men were physically fit and well. He also stated that both Jimmie and Joe were intelligent and articulate and defied the assumption that Australian Aboriginals were one step up from the ape.

Jimmie and Joe both felt vindicated.

'Doctor Ekstein may we ask one favour of you?

'You can, but I can't promise I'll be able to grant it.'

'We are, as you know, Australian yet we have been separated from our mates and are the only Australians being held at Zossen. We would dearly love to be reunited with our comrades at Senne.'

'I don't know whether I can help, but I do know some very senior officers. I can try contacting them with your request.'

'Thank you, Doctor, we appreciate your support.'

The two POWs were picked up from the museum and transported back to Zossen that afternoon.

They soon fell into the daily routine and although not in the same hut as before made friends easily.

Each day they hoped they would be transferring to Senne but notification never came. Finally, a guard approached them to accompany him to the commandant's office. The pretty secretary was still there typing.

Jimmie and Joe were summoned into the office.

'I have transfer papers for you both; you are being transferred to Senne camp immediately. Collect your things and be ready in one hour. That's all, dismissed.'

They were elated that at last they would catch up with Rob and Keith.

A troop truck pulled up in the camp's quadrangle, and the two POWs were ordered into the back accompanied by two stern-looking guards. It was not quite like the limousine trip to Berlin but the two Australians didn't care.

The journey took four hours, passing over very rough roads and when they arrived at Senna both men were sore and bruised.

The guards escorted them to their allocated hut. No other POWs were present as they were still out on work detail.

Deciding to have a rest while they could the boys lay down on their bunks and soon fell asleep. They were woken by the noise of prisoners returning from their day's work.

'Well I'll be fucked, we've got a couple of black blokes among us.'

Waking to the raucous banter Jimmie opened his eyes to see Keith and Rob standing over him.

'G'day you white bludgers. Did you miss us?'

'Bloody oath we did, get up and give me hug you black bastard.'

Joe joined in with backslapping and laughter.

'Geez, it's good to see you blokes again.'

'How'd you manage it? I thought the next time we saw you two would be back home, if at all.'

The two Aboriginal diggers recounted their experiences in Berlin and how the good doctor pulled a few strings.

The four diggers were back together, at last, and they spent their leisure hours talking about what might happen in the future.

'Hey Rob, have you thought about what you might do when you return home?' asked Joe.

'Yeah, I have. I saw a poster at the Tok H encouraging returned soldiers to register for the Soldier's Settlement Scheme.'

'Although the poster was for New South Wales, Tubby assured me every state has established a similar scheme. I'm thinking of applying.'

'What do you know about farming, mate?' asked Jimmie.

'Not much, but the government trains you and they allocate an expert to work with you initially.'

'What would you farm down there in Tassie?'

'I suppose it depends where the land is. It could be sheep in the Midlands or cattle for that matter. It could even be in the Huon Valley not far from where I come from. If that was the case I may even become an orchardist.'

'I must admit earning a living of the land sounds appealing,' said Jimmie.

'Well, you should apply once we get out of here.'

'I expect it depends also on who wins this fucking war.'

'Don't even contemplate that mate. We'll win the war and that's that.'

'What about you Joe? Are you going to go professional and become welter weight champion of the world?'

'Not bloody likely. I sort of like the sound of what Rob is thinking of doing. Hey Rob, you never know… we could be neighbours.'

'I'd like that Joe.'

'So that leaves you, Keith. What are your plans?'

'I don't know; I haven't given it much thought, to be honest. I worked on a sugar cane farm for a while; it's bloody hard yakka. Maybe if it were my own it might be different. I think I'll wait to see what happens with the war first.'

December 1917

The four Australian prisoners made the most of the Czar's hospitality. The commandant, Colonel Weber, gave permission for the prisoners to erect a Christmas tree felled from the pine forest surrounding the camp. The more artistic of the POWs made Christmas decorations. Tiny Peterson, a five-foot-nothing Englishman, was given the task of placing the star of Bethlehem on the top of the tree. Colonel Weber also agreed to the prisoners' request to have one of the searchlights illuminate the tree between the hours of six and ten pm.

Christmas Eve arrived and the prisoners gathered in front of the tree and sang carols. The men almost forgot there was a war going on.

Jimmie had taken on the role of Red Cross advocate and it was by his efforts that each of the men received a Christmas parcel.

The two Aboriginals were the only black men in the camp and it didn't take long for them to earn the respect of the majority of prisoners.

I Just Want to Get Out of This Place

Chapter 24

An Australian digger approached Rob in the exercise yard.

He was a tall man with a shock of red hair. His nickname was Bluey but his real name was Sean Jones.

'G'day mate, do you mind if I have a word?'

'That depends. Who in the hell are you?'

'Sorry, I should have introduced myself. I'm Sean, but everybody calls me Bluey.'

'Right, well my name's Rob. I suppose you knew that didn't you?'

'Yeah, I did. I want to talk to you about something that's very important.'

Bluey looked all around to ensure there were no guards within earshot.

'Me and the blokes in my hut want to dig an escape tunnel out of this place. I want to know whether you and your hut would be in on it?'

'Where do you plan to dig it?'

'Don't know yet. We're in the early planning stage.'

'Well, you better sort that one out, Bluey. I suggest somewhere where you can't be seen digging the fucking thing.'

'I gather from your tone you wouldn't be interested?'

'I didn't say that, but you've got a long way to go before you even break ground. In principle, if the boys and I think it's feasible we'd probably throw our hats in.'

'Okay, well how about we try to get together for a planning meeting without bringing attention to ourselves?'

'Mate, that would be bloody difficult. Why don't I broach the subject with my blokes and see if we can come up with a plan? You do the same with your hut, and you and I meet out here and compare notes.'

'Yeah, all right, sounds good.'

The two Aussie prisoners parted ways; later in the day just before lights out the two leaders introduced the concept to the huts.

155

'How in the fuck are we going to find a spot where we can start digging without being seen?' said Keith.

'Well that's the key question. If we start in one of the huts we may get sprung by one of those surprise inspections in the middle of the night,' said Rob.

'What about the amenities block?'

'Yeah, that's a possibility.'

'I don't know whether I told you blokes, but I approached the commandant to ask him if I could build a boxing ring in the yard. The idea was to have boxing matches between those prisoners who felt like a having a go.'

'No, you didn't tell us, Joe; bloody good idea but how does it help with our escape plans?' asked Rob.

'The key to not being obvious is to dig where it is bloody obvious. If permission was given, the ring would be a permanent fixture. We could cover the sides and have men digging under the bloody thing.'

'Bloody hell Joe, I think you've hit on something here. What a great idea.'

Three weeks later the word came down; permission had been granted to construct a boxing ring in the exercise yard.

Joe convinced the authorities to locate the ring close to the perimeter fence so as not to impinge on the soccer and Australian Rules games which had become a regular feature.

Even so, the men estimated that it would require a tunnel of at least forty metres to reach far enough into the pine forest for them not to be detected when exiting.

Work began building the boxing ring on March 1st 1918. The timber came from a sawmill close to the prison camp, and the canvas for the deck and sides were seconded from surplus army tents. They began on a Monday, and the ring was completed by the Friday of the same week.

The excess timber was stacked underneath the ring. The guards didn't seem to mind. This timber would be used to support the tunnel, ensuring it wouldn't collapse.

The first match was between Joe, the Tassie Devil, and an Englishman bigger than Joe but as it turned out, much slower.

It was heralded as a three-round fight but only lasted two, as the English corner threw in the white towel.

These boxing matches held twice a week were extremely popular with not only the POWs but also the guards.

It was agreed that four matches a week would be held based on demand. This doubled the tunnellers work time.

In the meantime, a working team was furiously digging the escape tunnel. Much of the soil remained under the ring but eventually, the planning committee decided they needed to dispose of the soil elsewhere.

Jimmie had an excellent idea.

'While the boxing matches are being conducted, the soil could be moved out from the bottom of the ring and then we could all spread it around with our feet. We know we have over two hundred prisoners in the crowd at any one time so a large amount of soil could be distributed. The guards shouldn't prove to be a problem, as they all seem to congregate in the one area.'

'Yeah. That sounds as if it could work Jimmie, worth a try anyway,' said Bluey.

The tunnel digging was well under way by April 1st and the committee estimated it would be completed by the end of October.

Jack Was a Ripper

Chapter 25

Jack Allan Irwin

December 1915

Another Aboriginal Digger still fighting on the Western Front at the same time Jimmie and Joe were incarcerated was William Allan Irwin known to all as Jack.

Jack was born in Coonabarabran in New South Wales, Australia. He never knew his birth date, as being an Aboriginal, his birth wasn't registered. He did know he was born in 1878. His father was William Allan Irwin, having the same name as Jack's, and his mother was an Aboriginal woman, Eliza Griffin from the Kamilaroi Nation.

Jack came from a large family consisting of two brothers and three stepbrothers.

158

His parents separated when Jack was young, leaving him and his two brothers to be raised by his mother and his stepfather. Another two brothers were born into the family soon after.

Jack was a true blue country boy; he loved the land and working with farm animals, particularly sheep. It was, therefore, a natural progression that he became a shearer working with his brother, Jim, shearing in sheds all over New South Wales.

The two Irwin brothers were finishing up for the day. Both had completed their quota of sheep.

'Jack, what do you reckon about this bloody war over there in Turkey? It doesn't seem to be going too good for us at the moment,' said Jim.

'No mate, not too good at all.'

'Have you ever thought about enlisting, Jack?'

'Yeah, I think about it all the time. I just think by the time I enlist and go through training the bloody thing will be over. That's about eight to twelve weeks of shearing out the window for no good reason.'

'Yeah, I see your point. I hope that doesn't happen to me.'

'What do you mean?'

'I've enlisted mate; I'm off to basic training in ten days.'

'Fucking hell, you haven't.'

159

'Yep, doing my thing for the country. Besides, I'd like to see a bit of the world, and I don't see myself getting another opportunity anytime soon.'

'You sly bastard. Have you told Mum and Dad yet?'

'No, I'm not really looking forward to it. I thought I might leave it to the day I leave.'

'Come on Jim, you can't do that. You owe it to them.'

'Yeah; I suppose you're right. Why don't you come with me… you know, brothers in arms and all that?'

'I'll think about it.'

'Well, don't think too long. I want you to be with me when I get shipped over.'

The two brothers cleaned up after the day's shearing and headed back to the family home around 5pm.

Eliza always had dinner on the table at 6pm; tonight they would all have lamb chops and vegetables.

Once the table had been cleared and the tea was brewing on the stove, Jim announced his intention to join the army. His mother and stepfather were saddened, although they were half-expecting it.

No sooner had Jim made his announcement than Jack also informed the family of his intention to enlist.

The thought of two of her boys going away to war was too much for Eliza to bear, and she broke down crying.

Worse was still to come as the youngest boy would enlist six months later.

'Bloody hell I didn't know you would decide so soon, Jack. Poor Mum.'

'Well, I wouldn't let you go off and claim all the glory. Besides, you're going to need me to watch your back.'

'Well, I have to say; I'm really pleased you're coming mate.'

'Yeah me too Jimmie, and don't worry about Mum; she'll get over it.'

Over the next week or so the Irwin brothers bade farewell to their mates and relatives. They caught the train down to Sydney where they would begin basic training. Army life would prove to be dramatically different from that of a shearer.

The brothers enlisted with C Company, 33rd Battalion.

January 1916

Army training began in early January. A typical day consisted of:

7.30   Parade without arms

8.00   Breakfast

9.15   Parade with arms. Inspection to ensure properly dressed and equipment is clean.

9.45   All platoons smart steady drill of a ceremonial nature.

10.00   Company forms up. Platoons march to the range. March discipline to be practised including halts, falling out, taking off equipment, falling in, and marching at attention.

10.30   Platoon shoots at improvised targets; glass bottles, cans etc.

12.10   Artillery and diamond formations rapid deployments speed at taking up fire positions.

12.30   March back to billets and dismiss.

        During this march, back by the platoons should march past the battalion commander and show themselves off.

1pm   Dinner

2.15   Recreational games

Training Leaflet No1 I.G. Training 1915

With some variations, this was the basis of the training program for the next eight weeks.

May 1916

Jack and Jimmie Irwin departed Sydney on May 4th 1916 on board *HMAT Marathon* bound for England.

EXCHANGE STUDIOS H.M.A.T. "MARATHON." 49 Pitt St. Sydney N.S.W.

The two-month journey included parades, drills, two-up and seasickness.

Finally, they disembarked at Devonport on July 9, 1916, where the 33rd Battalion marched to Durrington Army Camp at Lark Hill.

On November 27 they left Durrington to board trains, which would take them to Southampton where they boarded a ship bound for France.

The Irwin brothers didn't see action until June 7th 1917; the 33rd's first taste of battle was at Messines Ridge a major Allied offensive. The battalion was part of 3rd Australian Division, 11 Anzac Corps.

Some historians have said that this battle was the most successful of the entire war. If not, it surely was on the Western Front.

General Plumer was assigned to command the battle beginning on June 7th 1917 with the detonation of nineteen underground mines beneath the German lines.

June 1917

Name of Mine	Charge (lbs)	Crater Diameter	Dug By
Hill 60 A	53 500	191 feet	1st Australian Tunnelling Company
Hill 60 B	70 000	260 feet	1st Australian Tunnelling Company

St Eloi	95 600	176 feet	1st Canadian Tunnelling Company
Hollandscheschour 1	34 200	183 feet	250th Tunnelling Company
Hollandscheschour 2	14 900	105 feet	250th Tunnelling Company
Hollandscheschour 3	17 500	141 feet	250th Tunnelling Company
Petit Bois 1	30 000	175 feet	250th Tunnelling Company
Petit Bois 2	30 000	217 feet	250th Tunnelling Company
Maedelstede Farm	94 000	217 feet	250th Tunnelling Company
Peckham	87 000	240 feet	250th Tunnelling Company
Spanbroekmolen	91 000	250 feet	171st Tunnelling Company
Kruisstraat 1 }	30 000	235 feet	171st Tunnelling Company
Kruisstraat 4 }	19 500	(linked explosions)	171st Tunnelling Company
Kruisstraat 2	30 000	217 feet	171st Tunnelling Company
Kruisstraat 3	30 000	202 feet	171st Tunnelling Company
Ontario Farm	60 000	200 feet	171st Tunnelling Company
Trench 127 Left	36 000	182 feet	3rd Canadian Tunnelling Company
Trench 127 Right	50 000	210 feet	3rd Canadian Tunnelling Company
Trench 122 Left	20 000	195 feet	3rd Canadian Tunnelling Company
Trench 122 Right	40 000	228 feet	3rd Canadian Tunnelling

Flanders, Belgium 1916

General Haig was studying a report written by Major Norton-Griffiths, an engineer of high renown. Prior to the war, Norton-Griffiths had owned an engineering company that had built tunnels in Britain, South Africa and Australia. His company was given the task of blowing up oil wells in Romania to stop the Germans getting their hands on the precious commodity.

Major Norton-Griffiths

Major Norton-Griffiths had written a report to General Plumer recommending he and a team of engineers, with hand-picked sappers, tunnel under the German lines and fill them with explosives with the objective of blowing the Germans to kingdom come. This, he asserted, would allow the Allied forces to attack and take the high ridge of Messines thus securing the Ypres salient.

General Plumer requested a meeting with General Haig to discuss the plan. Norton-Griffiths accompanied him.

'So you think this plan will work do you, General?'

'Yes, sir, I have gone over it thoroughly with Major Norton-Griffiths and I am sure it will work. The major has extensive tunnelling experience and the methods devised by his company will mean the noise levels will be kept to a minimum so the Germans won't hear a damn thing, not until the explosions go off, anyway. They call it clay kicking.'

'How are you going to recruit experienced diggers from the ranks, Major?' asked Haig.

'Sir, I have hired many men in my engineering company before the war. I know what to look for and how to find them.'

'Plumer, I will approve this plan. Just make sure it works.'

'It will, sir, I assure you.'

General Plumer and Norton-Griffiths left General Haig's office and hopped into the Major's black Rolls Royce. The car was pristine when Major Norton-Griffiths landed it in France, but it was looking a little worse for wear now.

They were pleased that General Haig had approved their plan but were very conscious of the long hard road in front of them.

'So, Norton-Griffiths, how are you going to convince the various commanders to release their men to go and dig clay?'

'I think I know how to do it, sir.'

They arrived back at General Plumer's headquarters and agreed to meet the next day to finalise the location and size of the mines they were going to lay.

Once they agreed on the plan, it was up to Major Norton-Griffiths to recruit the men needed.

Norton-Griffiths (on the right) with his Rolls Royce

He loaded up the Rolls with several cases of Château Lafitte Rothschild wine, which he had collected since landing in France.

He then drove around to various units trying to convince the commanders to release men who had engineering or mining experience.

Norton-Griffiths pulled up at the command post of Major John Davies.

'Hello, Major, I was wondering if we could have a chat?'

'Why not, Major. Come on into my luxurious dugout,' he said in jest.

'I have a proposition for you.'

'Oh, and what would that be?'

'I need men with good mining or engineering experience for a very important mission. I believe you have two such men in your company.'

'Do I? And who would they be?'

'Corporals Smyth and Goodyer.'

'I don't think so, Major, they are two of my best men. Out of the question.'

'Well, may I suggest six bottles of Château Lafitte may encourage you to release them into my care?'

'You're joking. Where did you find those?'

'Well, you can find them on the back seat of my Rolls. Never mind where I found them.'

'All right, Major, you have yourself a deal.'

'Excellent.'

Major Norton-Griffiths used this tactic to ensure he had all the experienced men he needed for the project.

At the completion of his recruitment drive, he had enlisted many miners from Britain, Australia, Canada, and New Zealand.

General Plumer kept a very close watch on the tunnelling and after eighteen months of digging, the twenty-two mines were ready to detonate.

The objective of the attack was Messines Ridge, southeast of Ypres. The Germans had occupied the ridge since 1914. The British knew they had to capture the ridge before they could mount a much larger attack on Passchendaele, in what became known as the Third Battle of Ypres.

General Plumer and his officers had been planning this attack for over eighteen months; Plumer was a meticulous planner who left nothing to chance.

He commissioned the laying of twenty-two mineshafts underneath the German lines running along the ridge. The plan was to detonate all twenty-two simultaneously, at 3.10am on 7th of June 1917. Prior to the bombs going off, they would hit the Germans with artillery. They would then attack the Germans with infantry attacks. Tanks and gas would support the infantry.

Jack and Jim Irwin and their battalion, the 33rd, were an integral part of the attack.

One of the mines was discovered by the Germans and destroyed, while two others were detonated by the British as they were outside the field of the attack.

The Germans were also tunnelling frantically and on more than one occasion the two sides would encounter one another and deadly hand-to-hand fighting would take place many yards below the surface.

The British started shelling the Germans on the May 21st using two thousand, three hundred heavy guns and three hundred heavy mortars. The bombardment ceased at 2.50am on June 7th. The Germans knew the British modus operandi and sensing an imminent attack, rushed to their defensive positions, with machine guns manned and flares launched to see if there was any British movement.

There was complete silence for twenty minutes. The Germans were increasingly nervous, then at 3.10 am the order was given to detonate the mines, which totalled six hundred tons of explosives. Nineteen mines exploded.

The mines blew the crest off Messines Ridge. People reported hearing the explosions in Dublin and the Prime Minister of the day, Lloyd George, heard it at number 10 Downing Street. No greater explosion created by mankind had ever happened before.

Mine Crater at Hill 60

Vosges - 1915 - Mine Explosion

The effect on the German defenders was devastating. It was estimated that the explosion alone killed 10,000 men. The objective was taken in three hours.

The Battle of Messines was a great morale booster for the Allies and for the first time; the defensive German casualties of 25,000 exceeded the 17,000 Allied troops.

Once the last of the nineteen mines exploded, the 33rd, along with the rest of Plumer's army, were ordered to rush the Germans' trenches. They were hoping there would be very little resistance but despite the enemy losing so many men, the Germans were waiting for them. There were many instances of heroism but none greater than Private John Carroll of the 33rd, a cobber of the Irwin brothers.

John Carroll rushed the enemy's trench, bayoneting four German soldiers. He then noticed a comrade in difficulty and went to his assistance, killing another German. He then attacked singlehandedly a German machine gun team, killing all three and capturing the weapon. Later he rescued two of his comrades who had been buried by German shellfire by digging them out while under heavy shelling and machine gun fire. John was awarded the Victoria Cross.

Private John Carroll

Jack also made the enemy's trench and managed to shoot two German soldiers before being wounded. He felt a sharp pain in his right buttock and collapsed to the bottom of the trench. A digger close by managed to get him on his feet, and together they made their way back to their own line. Jim was already there to meet him.

'What happened to you, mate?'

'I've been shot in the fucking arse.'

'Geez, that sounds painful.'

'Course it's fucking painful.'

Jack was transferred to a dressing station before being transferred to the 26th General Hospital in Estaples for further treatment. His doctor made the decision to evacuate Jack to England on board the hospital ship *St David*.

Jack recuperated at the 1st Australian Auxiliary Hospital at Harefield for the next five months. On November 29 1917 he was deployed back to France to fight another day.

Jack was keen to visit Poperinge as he knew of its reputation for wine, women and possibly the odd song.

He, along with two of his cobbers Albert and Chris, arranged to spend a few days leave at the infamous town.

'Hey Jack, do you have any idea what establishment we should go to?' asked Chris.

Jack was regarded as the elder of the group. He had turned forty sometime in 1918 although he had no idea exactly when. Chris and Albert were twenty-five.

'Not a bloody clue but I don't think it will be too difficult. We'll just ask one of the diggers that have been here before.'

The three Anzacs headed to le coq noir (The Black Rooster), a popular pub with visiting Australians. Jack was prohibited from drinking alcohol back home but there were no such restrictions in Belgium.

As usual, the hotel was full of diggers in khaki, drinking, laughing, and having a good time. Jack went up to the bar and ordered three pints from the pretty barmaid. Once the boys had a beer in hand, they looked around to see whether they could spot anyone they knew. Chris recognised a couple of blokes from the 33rd and went over to say g'day. Soon after Jack and Bert joined them.

Eventually, after chatting for a while, Jack broached the subject.

'Do any of you blokes know a top class brothel in town?'

'Feeling a bit frisky, Jack?'

'Well, after nearly getting my arse shot off at Messines I thought it was about time I tested it out.'

'Fair enough cobber, I'd recommend Touche de Classe. I went there along with these blokes a couple of nights back and I can tell you I'm still not over it.'

'What do you mean still not over it?'

'I mean I still think about it every minute of the day. It was fucking unbelievable.'

'Well, that sounds good enough for me,' said Jack.

'Me too.'

'And me.'

Jack and the boys headed for the recommended establishment. They had no trouble finding it. There were soldiers milling around outside trying to pluck up the courage to enter.

There was no such hesitation for Jack. He simply knocked and opened the shiny red door. His two mates followed.

The reception area was very salubrious with a large crystal chandelier illuminating the room.

Behind a Louis XIV desk sat a beautiful mature woman with jet-black hair down to her shoulders.

'Bonne soirée Messieurs, I am Madame Phoebe. Can I help you?'

'Oui Madam, we are Australian soldiers seeking love,' Jack said.

Chris and Albert looked at each other. Chris whispered, 'very sophisticated.'

'Well, Messieurs, you have come to the right place. How long do you wish to stay?'

'One hour, Madam.'

'That will be five francs.'

The three men paid Madam Phoebe, who then led them into a lounge where several girls were sitting. After some discussion among themselves, the diggers chose a girl each. The girls then led the men to their bedrooms.

Jack had chosen a beautiful redhead by the name of Francoise. She held his hand and led him into an opulent suite.

'What is your name, Monsieur?'

'Jack. And yours?'

'Francoise.'

'A beautiful name for a beautiful lady.'

'Thank you, Jack. Where are you from?'

'Australia.'

'Really, I didn't think there were any black people in Australia. All the Australians I've met are white.'

'Well Francoise, the strange thing is the black people, who by the way are called Aboriginals, were in Australia many years before the whites came.'

'Really; how many years?'

171

'About 40,000 years.'

'Oh my goodness. I am sorry Jack, I hope I haven't offended you.'

'Not at all, Francoise.'

'Well Jack, I think we should go to bed don't you?'

'That sounds like a very good idea.'

Jack was a reasonably experienced man but he had never enjoyed sex so much. He promised Francoise he would return when he next had the opportunity.

When the three men met in the street they just looked at each other and started laughing.

'Have you ever?'

'Not like that, I haven't.'

'Come on, let's have a drink before we go back to camp.'

A Shot in the Arm

Chapter 26

1918 France

Villers Bretonneux

The year was 1918. The Germans knew they had to mount a massive offensive if they were going to win the war. Initially, the Allied Forces were taken by surprise because of the lack of intelligence, which was meant to come from the British High Command; hence, the Germans captured many towns and were moving on Amiens. The British High Command was fearful that if the Germans captured Amiens, the war might well be lost.

They quickly brought back the ANZACs from Belgium to be used as storm troops to be utilised where they were needed most. The first engagement for the Australians was at Dernancourt, which is located on the road to Amiens. There were 25,000 German troops against 4,000 Australian diggers. The diggers defended Dernancourt against all the odds and drove back the Germans.

The next village in the German sights was Villers-Bretonneux; they used mustard gas, firing canisters into the village, and opened fire with large guns. At nightfall, the Australians stormed the German trenches and drove the Germans out.

Brigadier General G. W. St G. Grogan. VC, of the British High Command, described this action as, "perhaps the greatest individual feat of the war".

The ANZACs then entered the village and fought house to house. The French and Australian flags were raised at last over Villers-Bretonneux at the cost of 1,200 Australian troops.

Many more were wounded including Jack who received a bullet in the right arm. He was invalided to England on April 9th,1918, aboard the hospital ship *St Patrick*. Upon arrival, he was admitted to the Pavilion General hospital at Brighton. He was discharged on August 28 and granted leave until September 11. He used his time on leave to visit the famous buildings and monuments in and around London.

Jack was dispatched to France on June 5th and on June 12 th he found himself once again on the front line. One consolation was re-joining his battalion and meeting up with Chris and Jim.

Once they got their greetings over and done with the two men demanded to know what he'd been up to in England.

'I reckon you get wounded on purpose so you can get away from the fucking front for a while, mate,' suggested Chris.

'Don't be ridiculous Chris; you try getting a bullet in your arse or your arm. I can tell you it's no fun.'

'I'm just joking, mate. What was London like?'

'Bloody good. I visited St Paul's, and Westminster Abbey but the best bit was visiting the Tower of London.'

'Well, it's good to have you back, brother.'

'Thanks Jim; I wish I could say it was good to be back.'

Bury My Heart in France
Mont Saint Quentin

Chapter 27

– Mont Saint Quentin
Fred Leist - Artist

The Battle of Mont Saint Quentin

August 30 1918

Jack Irwin was well and truly back in the thick of things as were his brother Jim and his great mate Chris. The 33rd Battalion would face the fight of their lives.

The rumours circulating around the troops were that it would be Monash's last big push to send the Krauts running back to Berlin.

'What do you reckon, Jack? Do you really think we're coming to the end of this horrible fucking war?'

'To tell you the truth, James, I don't bloody know but we can only hope and pray.'

'Well, if anyone can get us through this its old man Monash, he's proved himself time and time again,' said Chris.

'Yeah, he's pretty bloody good. I'd rather have him directing the show than any of those toffee-nosed pommy generals,' agreed Jack.

On August 30 the 3rd Division, including the 33rd battalion commenced their attack on Mont St Quentin. General Monash's objective was to render the line of the Somme River useless to the Germans as a defensive position and hasten their retreat to the Hindenburg Line and beyond. If this was to be achieved Mont St Quentin, a strategic hill, would need to be captured.

Monash was well aware that his troops were under strength and badly in need of respite; however, he needed them more now than ever. His regard for the Australian infantry was at an all-time high. Monash instilled in his troops the belief that they expected to win every battle. He knew they must succeed; he was concerned that if the Germans withstood the attacks until winter the war could drag on till 1919 or even beyond. Monash and High Command desperately needed more troops, but without conscription the likelihood of new troops in any numbers was unlikely. Politicians in Australia were also demanding that those soldiers who enlisted in 1914 be repatriated home, thus depriving Monash of his most experienced troops.

The attack on Mont St Quentin was crucial. The hill was less than one hundred metres high and heavily guarded, especially along the northern and westerly approaches. The 5th Division objectives were the Peronne Bridges and the village of Peronne itself, while the 2nd Division's was the bridgehead at Halle then Mont St Quentin. Finally, the 3rd Division, incorporating the 33rd Battalion, was to capture the high ground northeast of Clery, then Bouchavesnes Spur. Facing the Australian Divisions at Mont St Quentin were the 2nd Prussian Guards, an elite German formation that had orders to hold the hill to the death.

The barrage commenced at 5am. The German reputation for holding fast through such shellfire deserted them; the Australian force's reputation as fighters caused panic among the elite German troops. The 5th Brigade of the 2nd Division opened the attack, comprising of only 70 officers and 1,250 other ranks. It was less than one-third of its normal strength. The 2nd Division battalions to assault Mont St Quentin were the 17th, 18th, 19th, and 20th, all from New South Wales. The 17th battalion started along the Clery-Peronne road as the panicked Germans retreated to more defensible ground. The Australian diggers, numbering only 550 men, captured Mont Saint Quentin, a position the British Command considered impregnable. However, the 5th Brigade, having suffered heavy casualties, could not hold all its gains. The 2nd Prussian Guards Division recaptured the prized hill.

The 3rd Division attacking Bouchavesnes Spur had not successfully captured its objectives; this meant that earlier gains were threatened by German flanking moves. Monash ordered that, 'Casualties no longer matter. We must get Bouchavesnes Spur.'

The Spur was taken and the Mont St Quentin assault was protected.

On September 1 the 6th Australian Brigade seized in a second attempt the summit of Mont St Quentin while the 14th Brigade captured woods north of Peronne and took the main part of the town. The following day the 7th Brigade drove beyond Mont St Quentin and the Australian 15th Brigade seized the rest of Peronne.

The result was that three weakened Australian Divisions defeated five German Divisions. The action saw its fair share of heroics, with eight Victoria Crosses awarded. Twenty per cent of attacking forces became casualties. The battle was a true infantry victory achieved without the use of tanks or creeping artillery barrage.

The human cost of the Australian victory was 3,027 killed.

Jack, Chris and Jim were waiting with the 33rd Battalion in a recently dug trench. They knew it would be a hard fight, and many would lose their lives; they hoped they wouldn't be numbered with the unlucky ones.

Waiting for the Push

Their objective was Bouchavesnes Spur; General Monash made it clear to his officers that this objective must be won no matter what the cost.

The commanding officer, Captain Duncan, alerted Lieutenant Mclean the attack would commence in fifteen minutes. He in turn informed the men of the impending push.

'Well, it's not as though we don't know what we're in for. We've been fighting the Krauts for a good while now,' said Jack.

'That's true mate, and you more than most know what a German bullet feels like,' responded Jim.

'Bloody oath I do, and I can tell you now, I don't want another one.'

'How are you going Chris? You seem a bit quiet,' said Jack.

'Yeah, I'm okay, just thinking about home.'

'Mate, we'll be home before you know it; the word is if we can beat the bastards here they'll be running back to Deutschland like stung cats.'

'I hope you're fucking right.'

Lieutenant Mclean moved among the men informing them they would be going over the top in three minutes.

Nobody spoke another word; they remained deep in their own thoughts.

No whistle was blown to alert the Germans of their imminent attack. The troops moved quietly over the parapet and kept low.

They entered Road Wood using the trees for cover.

'Hey Jack, this isn't too bad. Maybe they've all pissed off,' whispered Chris.

'I wouldn't get your hopes up too much mate. They're probably just waiting for us to get into range.'

Just then a blast of machine gun fire came their way. Jack kept his head down but Chris wasn't so lucky. Several bullets ripped into his head, making him unrecognizable. Jack looked up to see his mate lying in a pool of blood, obviously dead.

Jack didn't think twice. He got up and ran for the bastards that killed his cobber, ducking and weaving trying to avoid the German bullets. He got close enough to throw two grenades and then ran into the nest, capturing the gun and two remaining German soldiers. Jim tried to keep up, but it was all over by the time he reached the German position. Jack instructed his brother to guard the prisoners and headed out again to capture yet another machine gun nest. Jack captured the machine gun with one hundred rounds of ammunition. Utilising the captured gun he ran firing at the nest, capturing it and its inhabitants.

Jack knew he was on a roll so he continued on his heroic rampage, capturing his third nest. It was when he was pursuing the fourth German position that he received a mortal wound. Jim alerted the medical team who carried him to the clearing station. William (Jack) Allen Irwin died from his wounds on September 1st, 1918, just two months before the war ended.

178

William Allan Irwin

September 7th 1918.

Private: 792 William Allan IRWIN, 33rd Battalion AIF. For most distinguished gallantry and devotion to duty during the operations at ROAD WOOD on August 31st 1918. Single handed and in the face of extremely heavy fire, <u>Private IRWIN</u> rushed three separate Machine-Gun Posts and captured the three guns and crews. It was while rushing a fourth Machine Gun that he was severely wounded. On his irresistible dash and magnificent gallantry, this man materially assisted our advance through this strongly held and defended wood; and by his daring actions he greatly inspired the whole of his Company.

London Gazette January 10th 1920.

Jack Irwin was the only Aboriginal to receive the Distinguished Conduct Medal.

Distinguished Conduct Medal

179

Other Australian soldiers demonstrated incredible bravery similar to Jack's. They received the Victoria Cross. Maybe it's time Australia awarded William Allan Irwin a Victoria Cross... 100 hundred years after he gave his life for his country; a country that didn't issue him with a birth certificate or allow him to vote. His descendants would have to wait until 1967 to attain those privileges.

Alby Lowerson

For most conspicuous bravery and tactical skill on the September 1st, 1918, during the attack on Mt. St. Quentin, north of Peronne, when very strong opposition was met with early in the attack, and every foot of ground was stubbornly contested by the enemy. Regardless of heavy enemy machine gun fire, Sergeant Lowerson moved about fearlessly directing his men, encouraging them to still greater effort, and finally led them on to the objective. On reaching the objective he saw that the left attacking party was held up by an enemy strong post heavily manned with twelve machine guns. Under the heaviest sniping and machine gun fire, Sergeant Lowerson rallied seven men as a storming party, and directing them to attack the flanks of the post, rushed the strong point, and, by effective bombing, captured it, together with twelve machine guns and thirty prisoners. Though severely wounded in the right thigh, he refused to leave the front line until the prisoners had been disposed of, and the organization and consolidation of the post had been thoroughly completed. Throughout a week of operations, his leadership and example had a continual influence on the men serving under him, whilst his prompt and effective action at a critical juncture allowed the forward movement to be carried on without delay, thus ensuring the success of the attack.

The London Gazette, December 13 1918

Robert Mactier

War Office, December 14th, 1918

His Majesty the KING has been graciously pleased to award the Victoria Cross to the undermentioned Officers, Warrant Officer, Non-commissioned Officers and Men:-

No. 6939 Pte. Robert Mactier, late 23rd Bn., A.I.F.

'For most conspicuous bravery and devotion to duty on the morning of the September 1st 1918, during the attack on the village of Mt. St. Quentin. Prior to the advance of the battalion, it was necessary to clear up several enemy strong points close to our line. This the bombing patrols sent forward failed to effect, and the battalion was unable to move. Private Mactier, single handed, and in daylight, thereupon jumped out of the trench, rushed past the block, closed with and killed the machine gun garrison of eight men with his revolver and bombs, and threw the enemy machine gun over the parapet. Then, rushing forward about 20 yards, he jumped into another strong point held by a garrison of six men, who immediately surrendered. Continuing to the next block through the trench, he disposed of an enemy machine gun which had been enfilading our flank advancing troops, and was then killed by another machine gun at close range. It was entirely due to this exceptional valour and determination of Private Mactier that the battalion was able to move on to its "jumping off" trench and carry out the successful operation of capturing the village of Mt. St. Quentin a few hours later.'

The valour and resourcefulness of Lt. Towner undoubtedly saved a very critical situation, and contributed largely to the success of the attack.

Are We There Yet?

Chapter 28

October 1918

Senne POW Camp

The tunnelling process was taking a long time; their hours of work were restricted by the duration of the boxing matches.

The tunnellers worked in almost complete darkness, and the smell, which greeted them each day, was of putrid stale air, dampness, and sweat.

The worst part was putting on their damp mud-encrusted digging clothes, which were worn in the tunnel.

They encountered several obstacles that could have proved to be fatal to the tunnel's completion, but ingenuity and hard work overcame them.

The tunnel was not much more than a rabbit hole, it was sixteen inches wide and twelve inches high. The tunnellers had to wriggle through, certainly not crawl. The tunnel could not be larger, as the amount of earth extracted needed to be limited. The requirement to dispose of the soil was becoming more and more difficult. Each digger was allocated one candle as they were very hard to obtain, so each man had to move along in pitch black until they reached their allotted location and then light the candle and begin digging.

As with any man-made tunnel it had to be reinforced with timber planks. The timber left over from the boxing ring build finally ran out. They began to steal the timber supports from their bunks. These came not only from the tunnellers beds but other POWs in the camp. Many a complaint was made, including by the tunnelling team, but the mystery of the missing boards was never solved.

Once the boards had been seconded and were in the tunnel, they had to be secured, which was an exhausting process. They had to be cut to the right size as the measurements differed along the tunnel. A tunneller would drag a board along the tunnel to the point where it was required. He would have to roll on his back, holding the board in place with one hand, and with the other hand wedge an upright board under one end to brace it. Nothing was easy about tunnelling out of Senne.

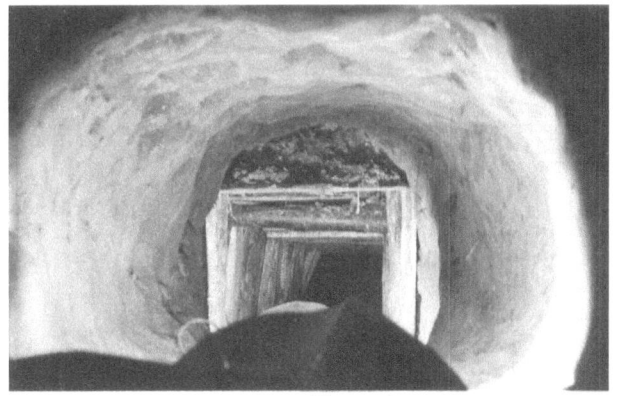

Escape Tunnel

When a tunneller had filled his soil bowl he would lift himself up as far as the twelve-inch ceiling of the tunnel would allow and pass it under his body. He would then tug on the rope to signal to the man at the end of the tunnel to haul it out. The soil would be shovelled into pillowcases stolen from the living quarters and stacked against the ring's walls. When the ring was full, the diggers passed out the pillowcases for the POWs watching the bout to distribute around the sports ground.

The boxing finished at 4pm, and once the POWs and guards dispersed the diggers would change back into their normal uniforms and crawl from under the ring, careful not to draw attention to themselves.

The roll call was at 5pm just before the evening meal.

November 10 1918

At last, the tunnel had been completed, the only task left was for Joe to dig the last few feet up to ensure they were far enough into the pine forest so as to escape without alerting the guards.

He slid his way through forty yards of the tunnel and began digging with a trowel, and after thirty minutes he broke ground. He made the hole just large enough for him to poke his head through. He was delighted. Pine trees surrounded him; he estimated he was three yards inside the perimeter of the forest. Carefully enlarging the exit hole, Joe slid out. This was his first taste of freedom in over a year and he was sorely tempted to just keep going, however; he knew he must go back.

On his return to the hut he reported his findings. The tunnel was still secure and the exit was exactly where they had planned.

The escape committee decided the following night, November 11th, would be the night of the escape.

The next morning at 9am all prisoners were ordered into the parade ground for a special announcement to be made by the commandant.

'Fuck, I hope they haven't found the tunnel,' said Rob.

'I reckon they would have demolished the ring if they had. Maybe he's going to announce he's going to double our rations.'

'Yeah, right.'

The commandant strode to his lectern and read a brief statement.

'At 11am today, November 11th, hostilities between Germany and the Allied Forces will cease. All POWs will be released immediately.'

The prisoners were bewildered. They just looked at one another. There was no sense of euphoria or excitement. The just couldn't believe what they had heard. Finally, a prisoner from South Australia, Bill Bryant, yelled out, 'You bloody beauty, the war's over.'

With that, all the prisoners were shaken from their daze and begun shouting and shaking hands and hugging each other.

'So what do we do now Rob?' asked Jimmie.

'Well mate, it's 9.40am. Technically we're still at war and we're still bloody prisoners of the Czar. I suggest we go back to our hut and lie low until 11am.'

'Yeah, I reckon you're right, mate.'

The men in Rob's hut returned to their home away from home to boil the kettle and make a pot of tea.

'I know this sounds a little crazy but after all the work we put into digging the tunnel I'm feeling disappointed we didn't get the chance to escape,' said Joe.

'Well mate, you've still got time. You could get in and slide and wriggle down the wet slimy tunnel, pop up in the forest and run for your fucking life until 11am. That should satisfy your desire to escape,' said Keith.

'No, you know what I mean, all the planning and digging… it just seems a waste.'

'It was a bloody waste and thank God for that Joe. In an hour or so we all will be free men; we'll be going home.'

'Yeah; you're right, Keith. What we should do after 11am is show the Germans the tunnel we dug right under their noses. That'll upset the bastards.'

'Yeah; I reckon we should,' said Jimmie.

'So how long do you think it'll be before they let us go home?' asked Joe.

'Geez, I don't know, I hope not too long,' said Rob.

'There must be plenty of camps to liberate. I just hope we're one of the first,' said Keith.

'What's the time, Jimmie?'

'Fifteen minutes to eleven, not long to go now.'

It was just like New Year's Eve back home; everybody moved outside to join the rest of the prisoners and when it reached 10.59 the whole camp started the countdown.

It was quite a spectacle; one thousand men counting down the last few seconds then...

11am November 11th 1918

PEACE AT LAST.

The Ex-POWs began to shout and dance and hug each other and even a few kisses were exchanged.

The German guards laid their rifles on the ground and walked away. Even they looked relieved that the war had finally come to an end.

The tunnel remained a mystery until liberation and by then the guards had been taken away in British army trucks.

The POWs didn't have to wait long. They were liberated on November 15th. Allied trucks drove them to Calais where they boarded a troop ship back to England.

The Anzacs stayed in England for three weeks where they could conduct some serious sightseeing, drinking, and other forms of frivolity.

Rob, Jimmie, Keith, and Joe boarded the HMAT *Ceramic*, the same ship that brought them over. This time they were bound for Melbourne. They endured the trip home without complaint despite the rough seas and an outbreak of Spanish Flu. Many diggers died from the mysterious disease, but luckily none of the four was infected.

Spanish Flu

Spanish Flu hit the world in the summer of 1918; the Great War was coming to an end with the death rate approaching thirty million people. When Spanish Flu disappeared in 1919, it had claimed between seventy and one hundred million souls.

No one really knows where Spanish Flu began. Some say China and others the Middle East. There is also conjecture as to why it was called Spanish Flu; again some say because of the high mortality rate in Spain and others say it was that Spain was neutral and therefore had a free press that could report was really happening.

The pandemic eventually had a disastrous effect on the Germans and its allies, inflicting massive casualties through sickness which they could ill afford as the British and its allies were having significant success on the battlefield.

The virus spread across the Atlantic to the USA via the military convoys. Many died on the ships, as the symptoms were a brief fever followed by death. The virus caused uncontrollable haemorrhaging that filled the lungs, and patients would drown in their own blood.

The reasons for the pandemic essentially remain unknown. The deprivations of a world war are held responsible by some scientists, although the virus similarly swept through non-war affected countries like the USA, India and much of Europe.

For example, four hundred and fifty thousand civilian deaths occurred in the United States. The majority of deaths were in the twenty to forty age groups. In Britain, some two hundred and twenty-eight thousand civilians died and four hundred thousand in Germany. Hardest hit, however, was India with a reported sixteen million casualties.

Each nation at war went to great lengths to conceal losses suffered through the virus, concerned that such reports would serve to encourage their enemies. In reality, each was suffering as badly as the other.

Curiously, in mid-1919 the pandemic withered and died abruptly without a treatment having been found. Scientists continue to believe that a repeat of the pandemic, albeit in a varying form, would find science as equally unprepared to meet the challenge.

HMAT *Ceramic* 1919

'What's all this panic about Spanish Flu, Rob? I've never even been to fucking Spain. All I know about the place is bullfighting and blokes wearing really tight pants and ridiculous hats,' said Keith.

'I'm not sure Keith, but the officers seem pretty concerned, I'm not sure why; I've had the flu before. A couple of days in bed and you're up and about again; good as gold.'

The diggers began to understand the severity of it all when two of their own contracted a cold then started to get symptoms of the flu. Twenty-four hours later they were lying in the ship's morgue.

'I don't get this, those two blokes who died, Sam and Dave, were bloody good soldiers. I think Sam won a Military Medal at Pozieres. They were with us at Gallipoli and the Western Front and survived. Now they've been taken out by the fucking poxy flu five weeks from getting home after four years away; how in the fuck does that work?' said Joe.

'I don't bloody know. What I do know, is I'm staying well clear of any bastard that sneezes or coughs,' said Jimmie.

'I'm with you Jimmie, I didn't enlist to fight for my country and put up with hell for all these years only to cark it on a rusty bloody ship on my way home,' said Rob.

There were very few surgical masks on board to help limit the spread of the deadly virus so the troops were instructed to use a clean handkerchief as a makeshift mask.

When the *Ceramic* reached Freemantle, Western Australia, more than three hundred cases had been reported. Commonwealth immigration authorities initially refused to allow the soldiers to disembark, as there had been no cases reported in Western Australia.

The government finally agreed to let three hundred of the most unwell diggers to be ferried ashore to the quarantine station at Woodman Point south of Freemantle. Many more soldiers died at the station over the following week.

To further exacerbate the dire situation, more than twenty medical staff became infected.

Meanwhile, on board ship where most of the men remained, conditions were said to be deplorable. A seven-day incubation period with no new cases was required to prove that the disease had burnt itself out, but new infections and deaths continued, caused by the cramped and close living conditions.

Public outrage grew against the refusal of the immigration authorities to allow all the soldiers ashore with casualties growing each day. Wrangling between the State Minister for Health and the Federal immigration authorities continued, and tensions increased to the point where the Returned Soldiers League made threats to storm the ship to ferry the sick men to shore.

After nine days of acrimony, and despite breaking quarantine regulations, the ship was ordered to depart in an attempt to defuse the volatile situation.

Another seventeen cases consequently were discovered en route to Adelaide. The remaining infected men were disembarked at Torrens Island quarantine station. No further deaths occurred, and after being given clearance, the surviving soldiers returned to their homes. A total of twenty-seven soldiers and four nurses at Woodman Point, WA, died of Spanish Flu during the crisis.

Welcome Home

Chapter 29

Hobart, Tasmania, February 1919

The *Ceramic's* first port of call was Hobart, Tasmania's capital. Constitution Dock was a mass of people, families, and sweethearts waiting anxiously to welcome their loved ones home.

Rob and Joe, the two Tasmanians from the group, were pressed against the ship's rail, scouring the crowd to see whether they could identify their families.

'I can see them, there are my mum and dad. I can't believe it I'm finally home,' said a tearful Joe.

Joe began waving his slouch hat, hoping to attract their attention. Finally his father caught sight of him. He grabbed his wife and pointed to Joe.

'Look Doris there he is, there's our Joe.'

'Oh my God it is him, he looks so skinny; I'll have to fatten him up a bit.'

'He hasn't even hit the shore yet, and you're already mothering him.'

'Hey Rob, can you see your folks yet?'

'No I bloody can't. There's just too many people. I'm sure we'll find each other once we are on shore.'

The Australian diggers began to disembark; finally, it was Joe and Rob's turn to walk down the gangplank. Joe made straight for his parents, leaving Rob to try to find his. Rob was making his way to the back of the crowd when he heard his name being called. He searched the sea of people but couldn't see his folks. Then he spotted his father waving; he was beaming. Rob made his way over as quickly as he could without doing injury to the people between him and his parents.

Rob hugged his mother and father, not letting go for a quite considerable time. No real words were spoken as they were all crying. Finally Jim, Rob's father, spoke.

'It's wonderful to have you safely back, Rob, we missed you.'

Norma, Rob's mother, was still crying but managed to say a few words.

'There wasn't a day or an hour when I didn't think about you and prayed you would safely return home son. I love you so much.'

Joe's welcome was just as emotional with lots of hugs and crying.

Eventually, Joe and his family made their way to the bus depot to travel back to the Huon Valley. The bus wasn't dissimilar to the buses that transported him and his mates to the front in France and Belgium.

Hobart to Huonville

Joe and Rob knew that after all they had been through together they would remain friends for life. Both soldiers had decided to apply for a land grant under the Soldier Settlement Program. They were hoping the farms would be in the same area.

Rob returned to the family home in Sandy Bay, only a few miles from Constitution Dock.

The house overlooked the Derwent River, a magnificent waterway about three miles across.

Derwent River Hobart Tasmania

They just made small talk on the drive back; there would be plenty of time to talk about the war and the past three years of Rob's life including his experiences as a POW, over the coming weeks.

Rob walked into the family home, the home he grew up in, to find nothing much had changed. His mother called him into the lounge room. As he entered about thirty family and friends shouted a loud WELCOME HOME ROB.

Rob was amazed and surprised. He certainly didn't feel like socialising but he knew they all meant well.

His uncle Bill initiated the first conversation. 'So Rob, it must be great to be home.'

'It surely is Uncle Bill, I was away for three years but it felt like thirty.'

'Reading the newspapers doesn't really give you a good understanding of what it really was like. Do you feel like enlightening me?'

'Without sounding rude, Uncle Bill I don't really want to talk about it right now. Maybe another time.'

Rob excused himself and made his way to speak with some other family and friends.

He warded off the usual, 'what was it really like,' and, 'how many Germans did you kill,' questions.

At last, all the guests left and the family was alone together.

'Why don't you get some rest, son? I'll call you when Mum has dinner ready.'

'Thanks, Dad, to be honest, I am pretty tired.'

Rob entered his old bedroom. Nothing had been removed or changed. It was a strangely comforting feeling seeing his football on top of the chest of drawers and the blue chenille bedspread on the bed. Rudyard Kipling's books were stacked neatly in the bookshelf, and it reminded him of the time he spent at Talbot House.

Rob removed his boots and lay down on the single bed. It wasn't long before he was snoring.

Two hours later his father entered the room and tapped the sleeping returned soldier on the shoulder.

'Wake up Rob, dinner is almost ready.'

'Thanks, Dad, what time is it?'

'It's six.'

'My God, I've been asleep for over two hours. I must have really needed it.'

'You must have. Why don't you freshen up a bit?'

'Thanks, Dad, it's good to be home again.'

'It's good to have you home, Rob.'

Rob used the family bathroom, the one he learnt to clean his teeth in and where he fell asleep in the bath making him late for school on more than one occasion. The memories of living in the house were flooding back.

He joined his parents at the kitchen table where a bottle of chilled Cascade Beer took pride of place.

'Can I interest you in a beer, Rob?'

'You bet you can, Dad, I haven't tasted a Cascade for years.'

Jim poured out three glasses.

'Norma darling, I know you don't normally drink, but I've poured you a glass so we can toast our boy's return.'

'I'll be in that, sweetheart.'

Norma had cooked roast lamb, Rob's favourite dinner. When they had finished eating and while Norma was serving the pavlova, Jim broached the subject of Rob's future.

'I'm sure you've thought about what options you have available Rob, but have you come to any decision?'

'Yeah, Dad I'm leaning to applying for a Land Settlement Grant. I know it sounds strange for a city boy to aspire to become a farmer but after what I've been through in the last few years I think it would be the right move.'

'What do you mean by farming?'

'You know, get a farm and work it until you can make a good living out of it.'

'That sounds all very fine Rob, but you know nothing about farming. Who's going to teach you?'

'It can't be that hard, Dad. You plough the soil, plant some wheat seed, watch it grow then harvest it.'

'Yeah, sounds like a piece of cake. So when are you going to become a farmer son and where's the farm?'

'I've already registered with the Closer Settlement Board. I am being interviewed next week, and all going well I should be working on my own farm inside three months.'

'What the hell is the Closer Settlement Board?'

'They're responsible for allocating the land and granting you a sum of money for living and buying equipment. They also organise training initially.'

'What, they sit you down in a classroom and teach you farming?'

'No, some bloke who's an expert comes out to the farm and analyses what you've got and what improvements need to be made. He also trains you up on proper farming practices.'

'Have you got any idea where they might grant you a parcel of land if you're approved?'

'I don't know until they approve my application. It could be anywhere. I'm hoping somewhere reasonably close to Hobart.'

'So, let me get this right, they give you a farm and give you money to equip it then they pay you a wage while you get it up and going?'

'No exactly, Dad, they lend you the money to buy the farm with a low-interest loan.'

'Ah, I thought it sounded too good to be true. What interest rate are they going to charge you?'

'Initially three and a half per cent then they increase it by half a per cent each year until it reaches the commercial rate. By that time I'll be making plenty to cover it.'

'You hope.'

'Dad, I thought you'd be happy for me. Here's my chance to be independent and do something with my life.'

'Don't get me wrong Rob, I am happy for you, I'm just worried it may not work out.'

'It'll work out, but thanks for your concern.'

Rob had already submitted his application with the Soldier Settlement Board; he knew Joe was intending to do the same. Both men received a letter four weeks later inviting them to attend an interview with the Soldier Settlement Committee. Ironically Rob and Joe were to be interviewed on the same day, Friday, March 12th.

Rob dressed in his best double-breasted suit, his only suit, and borrowed a tie from his father.

He decided to walk from Sandy Bay to Hobart, a three-mile journey. It was a cool day and he wanted to get his thoughts together ready for the interview; he went through his answers to the possible questions they were likely to ask. One question had him stumped. 'Are you married?'

He tossed up in his mind whether he should lie and say he was engaged but decided to be honest with them.

Rob arrived at the building that housed the Settlement Program's offices and climbed the single flight of stairs. He introduced himself to the elderly woman behind the desk and waited to be invited into the meeting room.

Fifteen long minutes later a grey-haired gentleman opened the meeting room door and beckoned Rob to enter. There were four men on the committee, all of them quite old.

Rob was asked a series of questions, most of which he had predicted, including the final question.

'Are you married, Mr Haley?'

'No sir, I'm not.'

'We're not insensitive men, Mr Haley; we understand you've been away fighting a war. I don't think we have a problem with your marital status.' He smiled. 'Well, Mr Haley, I think we can comfortably say you meet the criteria we are looking for. Despite your lack of experience, we believe you have the right attitude and an exemplary war record, which puts you in good stead. Congratulations; we will confirm your acceptance by letter shortly.'

Rob thanked them all and departed, barely able to contain his excitement. He couldn't wait to get home to tell his mother and father.

As he re-entered the waiting room on his way out he saw a very pensive Joe waiting to be interviewed.

'G'day Joe, don't look so worried. It was a piece of cake, mate. Just give them honest straightforward answers and you'll be fine.'

'So, you went all right then Rob?'

'Yeah, I'm sweet; they said I'd get a letter of approval in the mail in the next couple of weeks.'

The meeting room door opened and Joe was beckoned in. The same gentleman who greeted Rob with a smile now had a concerned look on his face.

White Australia
Black Heart

Chapter 30

Joe entered the meeting room and the chairman indicated he should take a seat at the long table. Four austere looking gentlemen sat opposite him.

'Good afternoon, Mr Hanson. I'm afraid there seems to be misunderstanding re your application,' said Mr Phillips, the chairman.

'Oh, didn't I complete the application correctly?'

'Well, no you didn't. Question three asks for your nationality. You answered Australian.'

'I am Australian.'

'You are an Aboriginal, Mr Hanson.'

'Yes, that's right.'

'Well, as I am sure you are aware; Aboriginals are not Australian citizens.'

'Maybe not in the true sense of the word but we habited Australia 40,000 years before your people arrived.'

'Yes, we understand that, Mr Hanson, but the Soldier Land Settlement act clearly states that grants can only be made to soldiers who fought for Australia and are Australian citizens.'

'So I fought for over three years, and was captured and imprisoned in Germany all for nothing. I have an excellent conduct record but after returning to my country of birth I'm excluded because I'm not an Australian citizen. Well, fuck you. You can all go and shove it.'

Joe rose from his seat, knocking the chair over as he did so. He stormed out the door, through the waiting room where two bemused applicants were seated, and out into the street. Waiting for him was Rob, eager to find out how his good mate went.

'Hey, Joe, how did you go, cobber?'

'They fucking rejected me the bastards.'

'What, why the hell?'

'Because I'm not a fucking Australian citizen.'

'You've got to be kidding me.'

'No I'm not. Because I'm an Aboriginal I don't deserve the same benefits of white soldiers – apparently.'

'Come on Joe, let's go to the pub and see if we can work something out.'

'Thanks, Rob, but I'm not allowed in a fucking pub either.'

'Shit I forgot. Well okay, let's go to the Criterion for a coffee.'

The two returned soldiers walked the block to the coffee shop and took a booth at the back of the café.

'So Joe, I've been thinking as we walked on the way here. What if you joined me on my farm? Mind you, I've got no idea where it will be or what I'm meant to be growing. Nevertheless, we could become a partnership of 50/50 the whole way. With two of us working it we should be able to make it work.'

'What do you think the Land Settlement Committee would say about it?'

'Those bastards will never know. Listen Joe, we've got to work out the details but what do you think in principle?'

'I reckon it would be great working with you, mate.'

'Okay, let's see what they come back with. I'm hoping for the Huon Valley but it's just as likely to be the Midlands or even up north, so we'll see.'

The two friends made their farewells, agreeing to meet again once the letter came from the committee.

Two weeks passed and Rob had received no letter. He was beginning to wonder if the committee had somehow got wind of his plan.

Finally, the letter arrived. He quickly opened it and scanned its contents; a grant of 250 acres of land at Cradoc in the Huon Valley had been approved. The property had been assessed as suitable for dairy farming and/or an apple orchard.

Rob was delighted; not only had he been accepted into the scheme he would be farming in the Huon Valley. His next action was to write a letter to Joe suggesting they meet at his parents' home in ten days' time.

Joe received the letter three days later and was excited about the prospect. It would mean he could continue to live at Glen Huon and make the daily commute. His parents had bought a Red Indian motorbike with the prize money

Joe had sent home with the intention that Joe would have transport when he returned from the war.

Joe made the decision to ride his bike into Sandy Bay for the meeting with Rob, and despite never having ridden a motorbike before he made the fifty-kilometre journey without incident.

He rode his bike down the steep driveway and parked it in front of the garage, utilising the only piece of flat ground available to him.

Rob, having heard the loud rumblings of the Red Indian, came outside to greet him.

'Well mate, you must be one of the only Aboriginals to ride a Red Indian in Australia.'

'Yeah, well the Red Indians and the Aboriginal people have a lot in common.'

'Yeah, I suppose they do. Come inside and meet the folks.'

Joe was always a bit tentative meeting new people but if Rob's parents were anything like Rob he knew it would be okay.

Rob led Joe into the kitchen where Norma and Jim were having a cup of tea.

'Mum, Dad meet my great mate and new business partner Joe.'

'Hello Joe, I'm very pleased to meet you. Rob has told us so much about you,' said Norma.

'I fought in the Boer War, Joe. I know how important mateship is when you out there putting your life on the line. Pleased to meet you.'

'Joe, would you like a cup of tea and a slice of chocolate cake? I baked it just for you.'

'Thank you Mrs Haley, that would be very nice.'

The Haley family and Joe chatted around the kitchen table for some time. The war wasn't discussed, nor the way Aboriginals were being treated by the government.

'Well mate, we better spend some time planning our joint venture. Will you please excuse us, Mum and Dad?'

'Of course, success is all in the detail and sound planning,' said Mr Haley.

The two returned soldiers went out onto the deck. Rob had an exercise book and a pen.

'Joe, I've been out to Cradoc and examined the property. What I found was 250 acres of which at least half was heavily wooded. If we're going to establish a dairy farm and possibly an orchard there's a lot of clearing to be done.'

'Well mate, neither of us shirks away from hard work. If we need to fell trees, we'll fell them.'

'I knew that would be your attitude, Joe. The first thing we need to do is make a list of the equipment and fencing supplies we'll need to get started. We need to get the board to approve our request and ship it to the farm.'

'I think you told me the Land Settlement mob will loan us an expert to examine the property and recommend to us how best to use the land.'

'Yeah, that's right, mate. I'm waiting on them to let me know who the bloke will be and when I should expect him. I'm afraid you need to stay low while he's there.'

'Yeah, I understand that.'

The two partners concluded their meeting; Joe made his farewells to the family and set out on his return trip to Glen Huon.

Joe's mind was full of plans for the farm as he rode along the Old Huon Road home. He decided to suggest to Rob that they name the farm *Talbot* after Talbot House in Poperinge.

The Rigger

Chapter 31

September 1919

Jimmie had been back home in Redfern for a few weeks catching up with his extended family and friends. Not much had changed since he left home to fight in the war. Jimmie's family, all ten of them, lived in Frog Hollow, an area on the boundary of Redfern and Surrey Hills.

Jimmie's Family Home in the Foreground

Although he enjoyed being in the area he grew up in, it was a rundown part of town. His ambition was to receive a land grant from the soldier settler grant scheme.

Jimmie submitted his application to the Returned Soldier Settlement Board just as his good mate Joe had done in Tasmania.

Jimmie waited impatiently for four weeks before receiving his letter requesting he attend an interview with the board committee.

He borrowed a suit from his next-door neighbour along with a pair of shiny black shoes and a striped tie.

On 25 September, he caught the train from Redfern to Wynyard Station. He walked the one block to Bridge Street where the Land Settlement offices were located. His appointment time was 3 pm.

Jimmie announced himself to the receptionist and took a seat. Five minutes later a distinguished looking man introduced himself as Sir Ian Grey.

The meeting room was dark and quite austere with a large portrait of the King on the far wall.

'Well, Mr Pearson we understand you would like to receive a grant of a small farm allotment.'

'Yes sir, that's correct.'

'Do you have any farming experience?'

'No sir, I do not.'

'Do you drink alcohol, Mr Pearson?'

'No sir, under Australian law I'm not permitted to consume alcohol.'

'Are you married?'

'No sir.'

'Are you engaged?'

'No sir.'

'Very well, Mr Pearson, the board will consider your application and inform you by letter of our decision. Thank you for your time.'

Jimmie left the interview with very little hope of receiving the grant he so badly desired.

By the time Jimmie had exited the boardroom, the committee had already made up their minds.

'We can't approve Pearson. He's an Aboriginal. We need to make out that he was refused for some other reason. I think the fact that he has no experience, and he's not married should suffice,' said Sir Ian.

They stamped a "Denied" on Jimmie's application form and began reading the next returned soldier's application. He was a white city boy who was not married. After his interview, he was informed that his application would be approved.

Jimmie caught the train home to Frog Hollow and went straight to his bedroom, a room he shared with his three brothers. He lay on the bed and began to cry. In all his time on the front, he did not shed a tear. He knew he would not be approved; his dream of working his own farm was all but extinguished. Then again, you never know, I may be accepted, he thought.

Jimmie just had to wait for the Board to decide.

Two weeks later the much-anticipated letter arrived.

Jimmie had no other alternative but to return to his previous job as a builder's labourer.

The following Monday, he caught the early train into Sydney and approached several building sites. Eventually, a company building a thirty-storey skyscraper took him on. He was told to report for work at 7 am the following day.

Jimmie arrived at 6.55 am, ready to continue the rest of his life.

He approached the foreman. 'G'day, my name is Jimmie Pearson. The site office told me to report to you.'

'Did they now, so what is you do, Jimmie Pearson?'

'I'm a builder's labourer.'

'Have you had any experience on high rises?'

'Yes sir, plenty.'

'How many?'

'About six years; it got interrupted by the war.'

'So, you were in the war, Jimmie?'

'Yes, sir, for three years.'

'Did you get wounded?'

'No, I was one of the lucky ones, sir.'

'My name is Tom; you can stop calling me sir.'

'Yes sir, I mean Tom.'

'Okay, I want you to go up top and ask for a bloke called Mike. He'll tell you want he wants you to do.'

'What floor is he working on?'

'The 25th.'

'Can I hitch a lift on the crane hook?'

'Okay, I'll let the crane driver know.'

Jimmie was used to working at great heights although not thirty storeys. Many a time he had straddled the hook and been lifted up to his place of work.

The hook was lowered, and he and another worker climbed on board, grabbing the cable with all the strength they could muster.

The crane began to lift them at a steady pace. Jimmie never lost his fascination with the Sydney skyline and the view of the harbour.

Sydney December 1919

The two men reached the 25th floor where they carefully stepped out onto a steel beam. They were then required to walk along the beam until they reached a fellow they hoped was Mike.

'G'day. My name's Jimmie and this is – shit I don't even know your name.'

'Mal.'

'Okay, now that we've got the introductions over and done with I want you two to go to the north side and hammer rivets for the rest of the day. I assume you know how to do that.'

'Yes; of course, Mike; we assume the rivets and hammers are waiting there for us?'

'Of course, they fucking are. I wouldn't have asked for you to do it if they bloody weren't. Now get a move on. We've got a fucking building to construct.'

Sufficiently chastened, Jimmie and Mal made for the north face of the building.

The days ran into weeks, which ran into months. Jimmie was feeling more and more despondent about his future. He'd received several letters from Joe and Rob, describing what was happening at Talbot and how encouraged they were with the progress being made.

Jimmie knew that as an Aboriginal without any rights his future was bleak. To make matters worse, he was having nightmares every night, reliving the horrors of war.

He was also suffering anxiety attacks, not just at home but on the construction site. There were times when he would freeze while walking along a beam. Jimmie knew he couldn't continue like this.

He made the decision to join the RSL, the Returned Soldiers League. He thought talking to other returned soldiers about their experiences might help his condition.

Jimmie approached his local sub-branch at Redfern and his application was refused. Despite the Aboriginal population being high in the area, the RSL decided that it would not be in their or their members' best interests to accept Aboriginal members despite their war service record.

Jimmie wrote to Keith in Townsville. Although the two hadn't communicated since they returned from the war, Jimmie hoped he might be able to travel up north and spend some time with his old friend.

Keith had changed addresses a few months back and didn't forward his mail. The letter was never received. Jimmie, in his mental state, assumed Keith didn't want to see him, which made him even more despondent.

Jimmie went to work on Monday, December 22. The day was the same as any other Monday although it was gloomy and dark with the promise of a storm. He rode the hook up to the 30th floor. The building was approaching its final stage with only the top floor to complete. Jimmie didn't have any particular plan in mind; nevertheless, the black warrior walked to the end of the girder and just kept walking.

Jimmie was a proud Australian, an Aboriginal whose ancestors arrived eons ago. Fighting for his country he put his life on the line time and time again.

How did the country show its appreciation for this soldier's service and dedication?

He was denied citizenship; he wasn't counted in the census; in fact, the government classed the Aboriginal people as a problem.

He didn't know his birth date because he was never issued a birth certificate; no Aboriginal was.

Jimmie was a returned soldier, yet he was rejected by the RSL because of the colour of his skin.

REST IN PEACE, JIMMIE

Talbot

Chapter 32

May 1 1919

Rob was sitting out on the deck talking to his mother about the plans Joe and he had for Talbot farm. Jim, his father, arrived home from the office and joined them.

'Good afternoon you two, I wish I could sit out on the deck all day admiring the view; I've got to work for a living.'

'Don't be silly darling, Rob and I have been discussing the plans for his and Joe's farm. By the way, we've only been out here for half an hour, not all day.'

'Just kidding my love. Well, Rob, you may be interested in this letter addressed to you. It looks official.'

Rob took the letter and opened it eagerly. After reading the contents he looked up with a smile.

'The Land Settlement Committee have approved all the equipment and supplies we requested.'

'That's excellent, Rob,' said his father.

'There's more Dad; they will provide labour to help clear the land. That was our biggest concern.'

'Well son, when is all this work due to begin?' asked his mother.

'Apparently, the supplies and tools will be delivered next week and the tree fellas will be on the property in two weeks.'

'It's all happening now, Rob.'

'Sure is, Dad.'

'So what's the next step?'

'Well, I need to get together with Joe down in the valley and begin preparing the place to accept delivery. I'll stay at the Grand Hotel for a week or so. He doesn't have room at his place to put me up.'

'Is there a shed on the property?'

'No Dad, that's the first thing we need to erect. We've got to have somewhere to store the equipment.'

Rob arranged for his father to drive him to Glen Huon where he met up with Joe; they had a lot to do before the tree fellas arrived, including purchasing a couple of tents. Talbot had a mountain stream winding through the property so fresh water wasn't a problem but food supplies needed to be brought in.

Three wagons pulled by magnificent draught horses arrived at Talbot loaded with fencing materials, tools of every description, kitchen pots and pans and even timber to construct the milking shed.

With Joe and Rob working long days the shed was well and truly finished before Tom and Pete, the tree fellas, arrived on site. All that was needed now was the 40 Friesian cattle the board had promised them.

Of the 125 acres that were wooded most of the gum trees had quite a narrow girth but there were some huge trees that had to be felled and cut. These trees would take a day each to complete.

Tom & Pete

The tree cutters managed to clear 75% of the wooded area by the end of their 30-day contract. Rob and Joe would fell the remaining trees over the coming months.

While Tom and Pete were hard at work, Rob and Joe completed the cattle fencing, encompassing 120 acres divided into 12 paddocks. Using a gate system the grazing area could be the entire farm or smaller allotments depending on the quality of the pasture at the time.

A condition in the agreement Rob signed with The Land Settlement Board was to complete the fencing before the Friesian cows would be delivered to Talbot.

Rob notified them of the completion of the fencing by letter, and the board responded, notifying him the cattle would be delivered during the week August 7th.

The final commitment the board made to all soldier settlers was to provide suitable housing on the farm.

Rob had not heard anything regarding construction of a cottage but decided to leave it for the moment. The tent would suffice for now, and the stream provided fresh water for cooking and bathing.

August 1st 1920

Rob and Joe were clearing some trees on the far side of Talbot when they noticed a Ford pickup entering the property.

'I wonder who this is, Joe.'

'Don't know, I suppose we better go and find out.'

'Don't forget, if he's from the government, you're just a mate helping out.'

'Yeah, I know the drum Rob, don't worry.'

The pickup drove over the paddocks towards them, stopping at the last gate.

'G'day, can I help you mate?' asked Rob.

'Yeah. My name's Frank Kirby. I've been sent here by the Land Settlement mob to help you out getting established.'

'What do you mean, established?'

'I'm a dairy farmer, have been for a bloody long time. I'll help you set up the dairy and give you the benefit of my experience as it were. Weren't you expecting me?'

'I knew the board would provide an expert, but the bastards didn't mention when or who. That's not to say you're not welcome, Frank. I could use all the advice and help I can get.'

'Very well I'll come back next week when the cows have arrived. When they get delivered hold them in the paddock closest to the shed.'

'Okay, Frank, I'll see you then.'

When the dairy farmer left Rob suggested they finish up for the day.

'Hey Joe, I joined the RSL; you should too. Why don't we ride into Huonville on your bike have a few well-earned beers and at the same time you could get a membership form. We could make it our regular watering hole.'

'Yeah, that sounds like a bloody good plan Rob.'

The two returned soldiers rode into Huonville parking outside the RSL hall.

When they entered the premises the president of the club, David Oats, apprehended them.

'Hello Rob, you're more than welcome but I'm afraid Joe is barred from entering.'

'What in the hell do you mean Joe's barred? He's here to sign up as a member.'

'I'm afraid we don't accept Aboriginals as members.'

'You've got to be joking, David. Joe fought with me at Gallipoli and in France and Belgium. He proved himself to be one of the best soldiers in our battalion. Now you're telling me that just because he's black you won't let him join the RSL?'

'I'm sorry, but they're the rules set down by the state office. Rob, I've known Joe and his family for many years and if it were up to me…'

By this time many of the members had left the bar to investigate what the row was all about.

If you don't let Joe join then I'm resigning my membership. I don't want to be part of an organization that discriminates against soldiers that gave their all in the war,' warned Henry Parsons.

'Me neither, I'll resign,' agreed Ed Wilson.

'Well, I'll bloody resign if the Abo is allowed to join. I fought in the Boer War and damned if I'll be part of any organization that allows black bastards to join,' said Archie Causon.

'Well Archie, it's been nice knowing you. Now get on your bike and piss off,' said Henry.

One by one the returned soldiers offered their resignation. David knew he had a major problem on his hands. Deciding to take the line of least resistance he caved in to the pressure.

'All right, I was only trying to do the right thing by you all, but it's pretty obvious you want Joe to be a fully paid-up member. So be it.'

There was one other hurdle to Joe's membership; under Australian law Aboriginals were prohibited from purchasing alcohol.

A plan was formed where a member could purchase a beer and give it to Joe. Joe would fix up the tab at the end of the night with those members who purchased the ale on his behalf.

Joe and Rob would continue the visit the RSL every Friday night after work until they both retired. Joe never drank more than four beers.

The Land of Milk and Honey

Chapter 33

Monday, August 5th came and went without any sign of the Friesians. Rob and Joe kept busy readying the milking shed for the new arrivals. Tuesday came, still no cows; however, what did arrive was the new milking machine the boys had ordered. It was meant to be the latest in dairy technology.

Milking Machine

Wednesday, August 7th

The two novice dairy farmers were trying to understand how the milking machine worked, as the instructions weren't very clear.

Joe heard a motor vehicle approaching.

'Rob, I think the first cows have arrived.'

'You bloody beauty! Come on, let's see what they're like.'

'Bloody hell, there's only six cows on the truck, what happened to the rest?'

The driver alighted from the cabin and introduced himself as Bill.

'G'day mate, shouldn't there be more trucks? We're expecting fifty cows.'

'I'll deliver another six tomorrow; I'm picking them up from Kingston. The rest of them will be herded along the road from Franklin. You should have them by Thursday.'

Thursday 8ᵗʰ August

Bill was good for his word; Rob and Joe could see in the distance their herd being driven along the Cygnet road heading for Talbot. Their future as dairy farmers was about to begin.

'Take a look at that Rob, what a wonderful sight.'

'It sure is Joe; they look magnificent.'

'Crikey, we better check the holding paddock, we need to make sure it's secure.'

The Friesians were herded into the paddock; the one specified by Frank. They all seemed pretty content, but Rob and Joe were quite apprehensive; they knew they needed to milk fifty cows that afternoon and again the following morning. Frank wasn't due to arrive at Talbot until lunchtime the following day.

The inexperienced dairy farmers were not confident enough to use the milking machine, and besides, they still hadn't worked out how to operate the thing. They decided instead to hand milk the herd.

The milking shed had twelve stalls; Rob decided that six at a time was more than plenty for them to handle at this early stage.

Rob and Joe began the milking. Neither of them had any real experience but soon got the hang of it.

They both knew it was imperative to drain the udder completely, or the cow would dry up in a couple of days.

Despite a few overturned buckets and the odd squirting fight the two men completed the task in six hours; two hours longer than what was considered normal.

At the end of the session, Talbot's first milk production equated to 500 gallons, a very good result.

Once the herd was safely back in the paddock Rob and Joe threw in a few bales of freshly cut hay they had delivered from the Huonville Co-Op. It was their intention to grow their own a bit further down the track.

They had hardly recovered from the morning's milking session when 4 o'clock ticked around; it was time for the afternoon session.

The same procedure was followed, bring the cows in, milk them for all they were worth and release them into the holding yard. Once all the cows had been milked they were released from the holding yard into the main paddock.

'I don't know about you Rob, but I'm absolutely stuffed. This dairy farmer business is bloody hard work.'

'I agree mate. I'm exhausted. I tell you what, I'll sleep well tonight despite sleeping on that bloody stretcher.'

'Yeah, I'm sure it's bloody uncomfortable. By the way, Rob have you heard what's happening with the cottage? I thought the board said it would be built by the time the cows arrived.'

'I haven't heard a bloody thing. I wrote to the committee a couple of weeks ago but haven't received a reply back.'

'I reckon you should go in to their offices and front them. They can't expect you to sleep in a bloody tent forever.'

'Yeah, you're right. I'll go and see them on Monday.'

Rob arranged to travel into Hobart with the hope he could get a commitment from the Soldier's Settlement Board to provide the building materials and a builder to construct Talbot Cottage.

He was successful; it was agreed that Rob would be able to move into a completed cottage by no later than October 31st.

Frank Kirby arrived at Talbot at noon on Thursday

'G'day lads, how did you go with your first milk?'

'To be honest Frank it wasn't easy, but we got through both sessions without too much trouble.'

'How much did you get?'

'About a thousand gallons'

'You did bloody well, or the cows did anyway.'

'Thanks, Frank I reckon it'll be easier when we use the milking machine.'

'Yeah, it should help, but you won't milk fifty cows with it. You will still have to milk some by hand.'

'Even so, I reckon we'll get through them a lot quicker,' said Joe.

The truck arrived with the building materials on October 1st, well before the scheduled date. The builder, Roy Halstead, turned up two days later. Rob and Joe helped with the build as much as they could between milking.

Rob's cottage was ready to move into four weeks later; a welcome change from the tent.

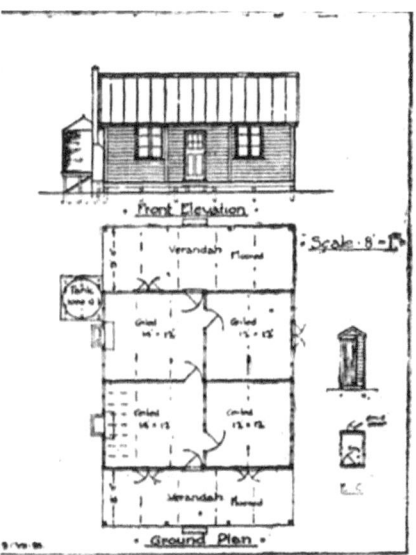

Standard Plan for a Soldier Settlement Cottage

Talbot Cottage

Rob and Joe proved to be a formable team; they fertilized the pastures, cleared the remainder of the woodland and created twelve additional paddocks. Four of the paddocks were used to grow hay, which meant they would become self-sufficient in feed.

The income from Talbot's milk production enabled them to purchase another fifty cows twelve months after establishing the farm.

215

The two dairy farmers bought additional farms, bringing the total acreage to 1500 acres by 1952.

Over the next twenty years, Rob and Joe became the biggest milk producers in the Huon Valley. They both married and had children. Both were regarded as pillars of the community.

Talbot Homestead
1940

North

Chapter 34

Keith arrived back home in late February 1919; he had no parents or siblings to greet him upon his disembarkation from the *Ceramic* at Townsville wharf. Both his parents died in a train crash in 1913, and Keith was an only child.

While the other soldiers were hugging and kissing their loved ones Keith, a solitary figure, headed for the centre of town. His objective was to find a suitable hotel where he could base himself while he sought suitable employment.

Before the war, Keith had worked on a large sugar plantation, not as a cutter but as a supervisor. His ambition was to find a supervisory role although he knew this would be difficult as he had been out of the workforce for the past four years. Keith had considered applying for a soldier settlement grant but had decided against it.

Townsville was where he decided to live which precluded him from re-joining his previous employer, CSR Sugar Refineries. They were located in Bowen some distance away.

Keith approached several agricultural-based companies in and around Townsville including Dalgety's, one of the oldest and largest rural companies in Queensland. He received a letter from the company's personnel department inviting him to attend an interview.

Keith arrived at the designated time and waited nervously in the waiting room. Eventually, a grey-haired man in a brown suit entered the foyer, introducing himself as Mr Jackson. He then showed the candidate into the interview room.

'Well, Mr Hodges, I believe you are recently returned from the war.'

'Yes, sir. I got back a month ago.'

'Must have been a terrible experience for you.'

'True, I saw and experienced things which I don't really want to remember. However, that's not easy.'

'Where did you see action?'

'Gallipoli and the Western Front.'

'Well I suppose we'd better ask you about your peacetime experience and see whether you could fill the role.'

Mr Jackson went through the normal questions he asked in an interview, noting Keith's answers down meticulously.

At the end of the interview, Mr Jackson thanked Keith and informed him that there were other candidates to be interviewed. He would get back in touch once a decision had been made.

Keith left the interview with no real feeling how he performed. He would just have to wait and see.

One week later a letter was delivered to Keith at his hotel. Anxiously he opened the envelope and read the contents.

In essence, although Mr Jackson was very impressed with Keith, a more experienced candidate was awarded the position.

Keith sat down on the bed and contemplated his next step. This was the only company out of the five he had approached that had granted him an interview. He began to consider moving to Bowen if CSR would give him his old job back. They had promised him they would when he had enlisted. The problem was it was a small country town with few prospects to meet a potential wife. Keith remembered the times on the front, dreaming of marrying and raising a family; that's what kept him going.

The returned digger decided to stay in Townsville for a few weeks endeavouring to find the right job – any job.

Keith was having breakfast in the hotel dining room when his favourite waitress, Lucy, approached him with an envelope that had just been delivered to the front desk.

Thanking her, he opened it and read the letter, which it was from Mr Jackson. Another position had become available. Albeit not as senior as the role he initially applied for, it was a good opportunity for Keith to get his foot in the door.

Keith was delighted. He was due to start at Dalgety's the following Monday, which gave him five days to find suitable lodgings.

On Friday Keith checked out of the hotel. Before he left, he approached Lucy and asked whether she cared to go out to dinner with him. She accepted enthusiastically. All in all things were looking up for the returned digger.

He began his new career as a storeman and over the following thirty years with the company he rose through the ranks to retire as Queensland Manager. Keith and Lucy married a year after their first outing and raised a family of two boys and two girls.

He never had contact with his brothers in arms again although it was not for the lack of trying.

The End

Epilogue

Wars in which Indigenous Australians have fought.

War	Year	Region
First Boer War	1880-1881	Transvaal, South Africa
Second Boer War	1899-1902	Transvaal, South Africa
World War I	1914-1918	Gallipoli & Europe
World War II	1937-1945	Europe, SE Asia, Middle East, Africa
Occupation of Japan	1946-1951	Japan
Korean War	1950-1953	Korea
Malayan Emergency	1950-1960	Malaya
Indonesian Confrontation	1963-1966	Indonesia, Malaysia
Vietnam War	1962-1975	Vietnam
Aboriginal people are Counted as Australians	1967	
First Gulf War	1990-1991	Iraq, Kuwait
Afghanistan	2001-2016	Afghanistan
Second Gulf War Iraq	2003-2009	
Peacekeeping 1947-present worldwide		

Source: http://www.creativespirits.info/aboriginalculture/history/anzac-day-coloured-digger-march#ixzz3sNN51aJO

Bibliography

Indigenous Australian servicemen | Australian War Memorial   https://www.awm.gov.au/encyclopedia/at

Australian Aboriginals in World War 1

Walter Christopher Saunders | Australian War Memorial

Indigenous Australians at War exhibition - Premier of Tasmania

ABORIGINAL WOMEN ON THE HOME FRONT: WORLD WAR ONE | Indigenous Histories

WW1 | Indigenous Histories

Aboriginal digger Miller Mack equal in courage, but not in society | The Advertiser

Anzac Day Coloured Digger march - Creative Spirits   http://www.creativespirits.info/aboriginalculture/hi

Extinction of Australian Megafauna - Humans and Fire

The Myth of the World's Oldest Culture

Megafauna extinction theories - patterns of extinction - Australian Museum

www.sro.wa.gov.au/sites/default/files/cpaf-namesindex.pdf

List of Indigenous Australian group names - Wikipedia, the free encyclopedia

Prehistory of Australia - Wikipedia, the free encyclopedia

Ancient Sea Rise Tale Told Accurately for 10,000 Years - Scientific American

www.kimberleyfoundation.org.au/uploads/41632/ufiles/First_Footprints_Press_Kit_-_S.pdf

Ice Age struck indigenous Australians hard - Australian Geographic

Ancient Sea Rise Tale Told Accurately For 10,000 Years - Study Confirms

Amazon.com: Buying Choices: Where the Ancestors Walked: Australia as an Aboriginal Landscape

Detailed record of the Ajabakan

Larrakia - Wikipedia, the free encyclopedia

Djabugay - Wikipedia, the free encyclopedia

3. Shrapnel Gully | Explore 11 Anzac area sites | Gallipoli and the Anzacs

The Battle of the Landing | Gallipoli and the Anzacs

Australian Light Horse Studies Centre

5. Shrapnel Valley | A walk around 14 battlefield sites | Gallipoli and the Anzacs

The History Press blog - Transport and supply on the Western Front

William Allan Irwin | Australian War Memorial

Roll of Honour: William Allan Irwin | Australian War Memorial

Battle of Mont Saint-Quentin - Wikipedia, the free encyclopedia

Battle of Passchendaele (Third Ypres) | Australian War Memorial

Rain and Mud: the Ypres - Passchendaele Offensive | Australian War Memorial

The Story of Talbot House (Toc H)

What is the 'Dreamtime' or the 'Dreaming'? - Creative Spirits

Aboriginal belief systems and spirituality - Biki

Cultural Aspects

THE DREAMING

▐ The Battle of Passchendaele - History Learning Site

ɴᴢ www.nzhistory.net.nz/files/documents/passchendaele-letter-len-hart.pdf

▌ Indigenous Australians at war | Department of Veterans' Affairs

▲ 1918: Australians in France - Prisoners of War | Australian War Memorial

? Indigenous Australian soldiers - World War I and Australia - Research guides at State Library of New South Wales

▒ Repaying our debt to Aboriginal soldiers - The Drum (Australian Broadcasting Corporation)

▢ Mont St Quentin and Peronne

▦ Families seek recognition for Aboriginal soldiers | Treaty Republic - Indigenous Australia Sovereignty, Genocide, Land Rights and Pay the Rent Issues

▦ Coranderrk - Aboriginal Farmers and Market Gardeners | Treaty Republic - Indigenous Australia Sovereignty, Genocide, Land Rights and Pay the Rent Issues

G Indigenous Peoples of the British Dominions and the First World War - Timothy C. Winegard - Google Books

▒ Anzac Day Coloured Digger march - Creative Spirits

▢ Dalgety Offices and former Warehouse frontage - Australian E-Heritage

▒ Indigenous Referendum Council named after drawn-out negotiations between Government, Opposition - ABC News (Australian Broadcasting Corporation)

▲ For Country, for Nation | Australian War Memorial

ACKNOWLEDGEMENTS

I acknowledge the 1300 Aboriginals who fought to enlist and fought bravely for their country.

300 died despite their country not recognizing them as citizens.

Preview Readers

Dr Anthony Dillon-Aboriginal academic

Kimberley Krarup

Michael Bell-Australian War Museum

BOOKS BY G S WILLMOTT

The Other Side of the Trench

Brothers in Arms

Escape

Red Lights on the Somme

You Forgot the Sauce

Survival

Soul Survival

Boy's Own War

Serendipity

Grand Deceptions

Children's

The Importance of Being Ivy